The Divine Child

The Divine Child

A Novel of Prenatal Rebellion

PASCAL BRUCKNER

Translated from the French by

Joachim Neugroschel

Little, Brown and Company

Boston   New York   Toronto   London

FIRST ENGLISH-LANGUAGE EDITION

The characters and events in this book are fictitious. Any similarity to real
persons, living or dead, is coincidental and not intended by the author.

Library of Congress Cataloging-in-Publication Data
Bruckner, Pascal.
    [Divin enfant. English]
    The divine child : a novel of prenatal rebellion / by Pascal Bruckner ;
translated from the French by Joachim Neugroschel. — 1st English
language ed.
        p.   cm.
    ISBN 0-316-11404-9
    I. Neugroschel, Joachim.   II. Title.
PQ2662.R763D5813   1994
843'.914 — dc20   94-17437

10 9 8 7 6 5 4 3 2 1

MV-NY

Published simultaneously in Canada by
Little, Brown & Company (Canada) Limited

PRINTED IN THE UNITED STATES OF AMERICA

For Caroline Thompson

God could not be everywhere at once,
so he invented mothers.

CONTENTS

The Divine Child

On her eighth birthday, little Madeleine Barthelemy caught a bad case of the jitters. She had left a plate of peaches in the sun, and they had spoiled. In decomposing, the peaches gave off a lovely fragrance, but they rotted all the way to their pits, secreting a black juice that wasps and flies were guzzling like mad. It was a dreadful revelation. At one swoop, Madeleine realized what lay in store for her. The eloquent putrescence spoke volumes. Her parents put the finishing touch on her panic by depicting the future as an evil territory to which only they could issue the passport.

Madeleine could never get rid of her jitters; they grew along with her, shaping her gestures and actions until she reached adulthood. Then her father handed her the invoice for her childhood and adolescence. It was a family tradition: these people did not give life, they lent it. Every child had to redeem it from his own genitors, paying off a mortgage that would invariably burden his descendants. Madeleine had ten years to refund an aggregate sum that could be increased and even doubled by a whole system of penalties. Making sure she left nothing to chance, she was simply observing the ancient manners and mores: they had shown their mettle. The past was a safety zone, where every trail was a beaten one. There was nothing equivocal about it. Madeleine barely left the house, much less went traveling: retiring every evening and rising every morning at the same time, she barely socialized. Since life is a trap, one must conserve one's strength while waiting for the end. Tomorrow was bound to be worse than today.

This wisdom, a brew of prudence and resignation, caused Madeleine to age prematurely. The way she shivered at the slightest coolness aroused disdain and snickers from her classmates. She was one of a kind in her excessive conformism, hence a not very interesting kind. She had no friends, she took refuge in her fear. Reaching out would spell compromise and thus doom. At eighteen, she was a melancholy girl with dark circles around her eyes, and skinnier than Olive Oyl's pinky. She was bypassed by adolescence and not illuminated by maturity. Only her black hair, a soft, bushy, curly flame, lent a smidgen of youth to her tight face.

A man, a distant relative of the family, took a liking to this innocuous little thing and courted her discreetly. His fancy was tweaked by the way she drew attention with her utter lack of distinctive hallmarks. Madeleine dropped out of school and married the suitor without asking herself whether she loved him. The notion of love was too fraught with uncertainties to merit the slightest consideration. On the day of her nuptials, the bride was lost in her veils like a fly in a cobweb. The groom's name was Oswald Kremer. He was twenty years her senior and an accountant by trade. Haunted by numbers, he converted every action of daily life into operations and transactions: he instantaneously totted up the molecules in a drop of water, the particles of dust hovering in a beam of light, the crumbs left by a torn baguette, the amount of energy used in his office by the end of each day. He agreed to assume Madeleine's debt, and he pinpointed the full amount down to the last penny, hour by hour, for the next ten years. He was truly possessed with a mathematical itch, and in just a couple of weeks after his wedding he had already found his wife's equation: he was able to give the weight of her spleen, her kidneys, her liver, her bowels, and to gauge her average heartbeat over a twenty-four-hour period, and he also knew everything down to the circumference of her every last beauty spot and the diameter of her every last hair. Aside from this proclivity, he was an obliging, loving man, willing to do anything to please his young wife, admiring as he did her reserve and discretion.

Fear does not kill, it interferes with living. Barely married, Madeleine cooped herself up in her condition. She was a scrupulous housekeeper who prepared dinner while waiting for her husband to come home. Having been a well-behaved little girl and a nerdy teenager, she was now a model wife. Except for one detail: she dreaded the conjugal corvée and grew more and more panicky as bedtime approached. How revolting for a man to sneak into her like a thief, crush her under his naked body, whisper into her ear, and use these diversions to deposit something in her belly: a gooey little souvenir that would eventually take up an inordinate space. Nothing could be more sickening. For months she held Oswald at bay and slept in a different room. She was repulsed by the slightest physical contact, even a caress on her hand. A kiss was tantamount to rape. When Oswald persevered, she would shudder and black out. He was patient, begging and begging for his rights, and in the end he had to wait six months to consummate the marriage. It was a horrendous ordeal: however much he apologized, however much he cursed nature for inflicting such contortions upon human beings, she remained frozen, biting her lips until they bled. He visited her two nights in a row; then, discouraged by her iciness, he did not dare repeat his offense. He consoled himself by calculating the energy expended in these exercises, the number of spermatozoa abandoned in Madeleine, and the rate at which his stock would be replenished.

As scary as coupling was the prospect of motherhood for the young missus. Pregnancy meant opening the door a crack to the unknown, which would then barge all the way in. It meant telling the unknown, "C'mon in, I'm all yours, ravage me." Not to mention the risks of bearing and the hazards of rearing. And besides, did she have the right to take a creature even more fragile than she and drag it into the chaos? If she absolutely had to breed, then she would prefer being inseminated by a great savant — say, a Nobel Prize winner, an elite mind. But the sale of Nobel semen had been outlawed after the demise of a laureate in nuclear physics had provoked painful squabbles. On his hospital deathbed, this Irishman was stormed by fanatics trying to extort the final precious drops of his mother liquor. Surprised by a nurse, they cut the dying man's genitals off and sliced them up before taking French leave. Ever since, all the Nobel laureates, whatever their discipline, have sported thick chastity belts, which they never remove, not even at night.

As if an ironic deity were straining his ingenuity to throw her into the very thing that she was fleeing, Madeleine scored a positive result on a pregnancy test. Insult to injury: she found it appalling that childbirth was a lottery ruled by mysterious genetic combinations and that you couldn't select your progeniture like an item in a department store. Abortion went against the grain of custom, and so she found herself in a deep blue funk. There was no question of her dispatching a mini man into the world and not fitting him out with all possible advantages and diplomas as a suit of armor against happenstance. But how could she accord him a non-negotiable privilege enjoyed by neither kings nor Croesi? How could she turn him into a crème above all other crèmes, make him absolutely superior to all his future comrades? Madeleine mused and mulled, goaded by the urgency. Every passing minute was a lost opportunity. Then, all at once, it hit her!

A brainstorm, yet simple: she was amazed that no one else had ever come up with it. She would skip way ahead: instead of moronically waiting until her little shaver was six years old to send him to school, she would begin instructing him as of the earliest weeks of pregnancy. She had to act now, without procrastinating until birth; everything is clinched during the days, perhaps hours following conception. She would not put up with having a little good-for-nothing mooching inside her for nine months without doing anything. She would be both mother and tutor at once, transforming her interior into a classroom. However, she needed assistance to see her plans through. Oswald, lost in his counting, was no help; and since she hated the thought of asking her parents for anything whatsoever, she discreetly unburdened herself to her gynecologist, Dr. Fontane.

This affable, slightly nearsighted middle-aged man with graying hair preferred the joys of conversation to the demands of medicine. He had embraced his career with a sort of youthful altruism that had failed to stand up to the monotony of the body and its pathologies. Examining his patients with great reluctance, he was eager to resume dialogue, so that speech would efface his concession to the organic. A bachelor — too many fertile bellies had cured him of any desire to procreate — he lived with his sister, Martha, a sickly, panicky old maid who was always ready to weep at the drop of a hat. Just as there are people who abuse their strength, so, too, Martha abused her lacrimal glands: the least little thing would unleash a crying jag — nightfall, a broken glass, an object slipping from her hands. She tried to drag people into the kingdom of everlasting sorrow, detecting in each person zones of distress that could produce sobs. Brother and sister, sharing the same apartment, had never been apart.

That day, when Madeleine revealed her plans to Fontane, the physician tried the gentle art of dissuasion. She was not the first woman to indulge in such fantasies. There were all sorts of more or less reliable methods to stimulate the fetal abilities in utero: they ranged from practicing haptonomy (hand language) to attaching sound belts on the mother's midriff. But none of these approaches came up to his expectations. Truth to tell, he found the whole business preposterous: a tiny being absorbed in its development does not have the physical capacity for learning. This rebuff, far from knocking the wind out of Madeleine's sails, buttressed her decision. It made her all the more determined, so that without wasting another second she launched into her teaching program. Having read somewhere that the mothers of Einstein and Oppenheimer had sung three hours a day during their pregnancies, she made a habit of crooning traditional ballads and old French folk ditties. She haunted museums to ogle at the masterpieces of painting and sculpture, and she spent her evenings listening to great music. Sometimes she would pause in the street to peer at a pretty girl or a handsome man, imbuing herself with their charms. On the other hand, she avoided cripples, hunchbacks, and tramps, abstained from watching violent movies on TV, and thought only positive thoughts. Every day, she would pick up grade school primers and force herself to read them in a loud, clear voice, hoping to instill the rudiments of learning in the future pupil buried inside her. Finally, by tapping the tip of a pencil on her teeth, she sent him encouraging Morse code messages that said "Whatever you may be, boy or girl, I love you, you are already the best."

Since all these efforts were on a very small scale, she decided to move up to a higher level. Deliberately neglecting the procedures charted by Dr. Fontane, she worked out her own system of education. She purchased some costly equipment, which she used as follows: inside each of her orifices (including those that common decency prevents me from itemizing), she planted miniature speakers connected to a multitrack deck that could play seven recorded tapes at once. In front, a wire transmitted the basic concepts of algebra and geometry; in back, she relayed language lessons, alternating English — "My tailor is rich" — with German — "Der Tee ist gut." Her esophagus was infiltrated by the rudiments of history and geography, while on her abdomen two suction-gripped speakers tirelessly recited the great classics of world literature. And above it all, Madeleine caroled and chatted through a megaphone aimed at her navel, convinced as she was that a permanent linguistic soaking would have the finest impact on her little darling. It was a complex installation that was coercive in certain respects, obliging her to perform all manner of stunts. Madeleine gladly knuckled under to these tortures while Oswald was at work; no sacrifice was too huge to turn her child into an exceptional being.

Nevertheless, her obstinacy could not wipe out a certain handicap: she would never reach her goal by herself in this condition of marital semisecrecy. An ally was of the essence. Swallowing her pride, she went back to Dr. Fontane, coaxing and begging him. Moved by the young woman's tenacity, he cudgeled his brain. Fontane was bored at the hospital, where he was head physician: he was tired of the intimate problems of his patients; the paltry plumbing of the large and small intestines had excreted all their secrets to him. He hated the fact that the anonymous force known as "life" oversees the shaping of our minds, our ideas. Why not short-circuit nature, browbeat it into speeding up its rhythms? And since he dreamed of leaving the narrow circle of his competence and soaring toward something grander and vaster, he saw Madeleine Kremer's offer as the finger of fate. Moreover, she was an ideal guinea pig — both ignorant and willing. Out of curiosity, Fontane set up an informal meeting of a team of his friends — a pediatrician, a pharmacologist, a neurobiologist, an obstetrician — and he bluntly asked them: Can an embryo be inculcated with the fundaments of education — reading, writing, and arithmetic — without any damage to its physical integrity? The response of the participants was unanimous: No way! Would they nevertheless care to engage in research along this line? No, it was a waste of time.

Fontane did not belabor the point: he had come up against the same skepticism that he had initially shown Madeleine Kremer. But he swore to himself that he would try. Without his quite realizing it, Madeleine had awakened his enterprising spirit, which he had lost since his student days. Beyond this aberration, he sensed a treasure, a gold mine, and within months he might be able to show his colleagues the error of their ways, their lack of boldness. His faith in himself was restored, and he embarked on this venture with an ardor that staggered and flabbergasted his sister, who appealed to his common sense over and over and was already foreboding the worst. Nonetheless, he succeeded in persuading her to collaborate, and he also engaged the services of a male nurse and a female lab assistant in whom he had complete confidence.

Fontane promised Madeleine he would devote himself exclusively to her baby (who would get a decisive head start over anyone else), and he buckled down to his task with the greatest discretion: so many researchers were already delving into prenatal education! Above all, no one must breathe a word to the grandparents or the father: the former because they were too authoritarian, and the latter because he had already performed his reproductive duty; what came now was outside his jurisdiction.

Part One

One

⌒

THE UTERINE REPUBLIC

For all his raptures, Fontane had not worked out a miraculous solution within a few days. He contented himself with some simple chemical bricolage: he decided to inject a cocktail of hormones, endorphins, and amino acids into Madeleine in order to activate the little creature's cerebral functions before his brain even came into existence. Traveling the warm, dark periplasts of the arterial system and the placental barrier, the liquid was supposed to accelerate the construction of a foundation for the tot's encephalon; this would trigger an instant assimilation of the notions transmitted by the mother. It was a rough technique with a complex objective, and Fontane fretted and fumed about it.

He was toying with a far more ambitious but momentarily unfeasible idea: to inscribe items of knowledge directly into thought just as one cuts music into a record. He would first reduce all scholarly matter to chemical formulas and then instill them in the subject, either through the blood with

15

medications or by ultrasound. The information would be home-delivered, as it were, to the cortical zones. And just as a whole meal can be compressed into a pill, so, too, Fontane pictured the invention of automatic learning in the guise of capsules or tablets. Eventually it should be possible to condense an entire education, from kindergarten through high school, into a single molecule and inject it into the testicles of the future father or the ovaries of the future mother. This would remove a constant source of human misery: the obligation to start at ground zero with each new generation. The encounter between an enriched sperm cell and an enriched ovum would produce a very high-level graduate. What progress! What a marvelous way of finally ensuring equal opportunity!

In the meantime, Fontane was reduced to perfusing Madeleine four hours a day in his office. The young woman, who had moved her paraphernalia there, forced herself to read aloud whatever was played by the cassettes broadcasting inside her. Devoting all her zeal to this preliminary aid, she kept reiterating how absurd and immoral it was to let Baby live the life of Riley inside Mom: nine months of leisure cannot be made up for, and such idleness leads to a lifetime of bad habits. These experiments continued until her third month of pregnancy. The treatment did wonders for the mother: after refurbishing her memory, she could reel off all the European capitals as well as the average flow of the ten largest rivers in the world. But the little schoolboy held his tongue. There was not the slightest sign of intelligence or sympathy from him, whereas he had already reached the equivalent of the sixth grade, at least in theory.

16

Nothing indicated that the cognitive processes had been at all awakened, so Fontane, with Madeleine's consent, decided to suspend the drip and the lessons. It was better to give up: his aim had been too high; the laws of growth cannot be violated so easily.

But then one evening the mom-to-be, disheartened and miserable about birthing a garden-variety larva, was counting sheep when all at once she was alarmed by a faint voice rising through her backbone: "More, more!" It was like a murmur, a vague quiver shooting up her spine and fading inside her ear. Had she dreamed it? She was alone; Oswald was asleep in another room. So the voice must have come from the pit of her stomach. Now it sounded like two voices twanging and begging: "More, more!" Caught unawares, she replied, "Right away," switched on the light, slipped into a robe, hurried into the parlor, and grabbed the first book she saw. Enunciating very distinctly, she read aloud a chapter on natural history: it detailed the delicate passage from *Homo habilis* to *Homo erectus*, and then all the way to *Homo faber* and *Homo sapiens sapiens*. Gathering anything that she chanced to touch, she next devoured a dozen fables by La Fontaine, a fragment of *Baedeker's Italy* — and when her husband surprised her at daybreak, she was exhaustedly stammering sentences from *The Practical Manual of City Gardening*.

It was only after Oswald left that it dawned on her: she had made out two voices. Two overlapping voices. Either there had been an echo or — an exhilarating thought — she was carrying twins. Beside herself at the mere idea of it, she rang up the doctor. His doubts notwithstanding, Fontane took a sonogram, which confirmed the mother's inklings: she was probably harboring both a boy and a girl, even though it was a bit too early to say for sure. In her enthusiasm, Madeleine promptly baptized them Louis and Céline, and Oswald acquiesced. The mother was radiant with happiness: a twosome would double the opportunities. In case one baby left the track, the other would grab the torch. Fontane, a wee bit vexed at not being the first to detect the twofold pregnancy, agreed to review the problem thoroughly. If Louis and Céline (for those were their names henceforth) could already speak in the third month of their prenatal lives (an exploit unique in the annals of mankind), then the enterprise would have to be relaunched on a vaster scale.

Fontane and his collaborators hesitated: not only would they have to offer the tots both a scientific and a literary training, they would also have to give them a smattering of music and the plastic arts, as well as make them aware of the great disciplines of anthropology and sociology. Madeleine could not take this burden on her own shoulders: having no grasp of such complex notions as set theory or the theory of probability, she might easily lead the cherubs astray. Hence, the approach had to be changed on the spot. And there was only one method that combined speed with precision: cybernetics. Since each passing day brought the pregnancy closer to term, the doctor hospitalized Madeleine in a room on his ward, telling her husband and the authorities that she had to remain in bed because of a risk of miscarriage. Next, with the dexterity that had astonished his sister, Martha, since their youth, he performed a delicate maneuver. By means of a transabdominal tap, he introduced a slender cable into the amnion; the end of the cable branched into two sliding clamps, which he attached with infinite caution to Louis's and Céline's minuscule auditory organs. The cable was then connected to a computer, whose synthetic voice declaimed the thirty volumes of the *Universal Encyclopedia* nonstop and in sequence.

Instead of following the school curricula in detail, Fontane had decided to supply the tots with knowledge in bulk, knowledge at wholesale, by delivering it alphabetically. It would be their job to sort through it once the articles were recorded in their minds as if on a magnetic tape. To avoid any hint of male chauvinism, it was agreed that Louis and Céline would receive the exact same treatment and not suffer from the gender distinctions that had been so discriminatory toward women in centuries past. However, a double danger loomed: the brains of the recipients could explode under the weight of this great intellectual baggage; or, under this enormous pressure, the small fry might soon endure an enlargement of their encephalons. For they would be carrying the workload generally required of a teenager in the pink, while each fetus was still dwelling in a mere cockleshell and their heads were the size of tiny plums. To stave off any risk of accident, Fontane limited their regimen to two volumes a week, which nevertheless added up to fifteen hundred pages — over seven thousand entries — not counting diagrams and illustrations.

Fontane also succeeded in placing two microchips on the twins' parietal lobes — two silicon chips that would supposedly gear up their cerebral potential: it was like grafting on extra meninges. To help the tots absorb the more difficult subject matter, he injected into their umbilical cords all kinds of sugary goodies flavored with mint and menthol, orange, lemon, and lime; which the little tykes, like all babies, were bound to adore. Madeleine, for her part, continued reading aloud some of the texts being dispatched to her children. Unable to keep up with the computer's speed, she usually read without comprehending; she was still on the first letter in the first volume of the encyclopedia (to be very precise, the article on "Amputation") when the peewees had already digested four volumes. And it took all of Fontane's blandishments, plus a few threats of sobs from Martha, to get Madeleine to give up the speakers in her mouth and a few other choice places.

Still jubilant despite the discomfort of her position, she soon forgot all about those crude makeshifts. She swelled with pride at the thought that she was manufacturing in her own factory two miracles of cognition, next to whom Euclid, Newton, and Pierre and Marie Curie would look like retards. Louis and Céline would embody an unprecedented type of humanity that would send even their most illustrious predecessors back to the Stone Age. Since there was scant likelihood that any other mom in any other clinic was concurrently involved in an identical experiment, Madeleine's babies would have no rivals. Dr. Fontane, however, was far from sharing her optimism. As he explained to Martha, there was no certainty that the siblings would be born intelligent, if intelligence is the capacity for separating, discriminating, but also tying together different realities. The tots were enduring such a huge cranial cramming that they would at most belch out a helter-skelter torrent of information, like parrots. They would become sinkholes of idiot-savantery — knowing, for instance, the colors of every single flag in the world, yet remaining utterly incapable of hammering in a nail or unscrewing a light bulb. On the other hand, there was no guarantee that they would weather the experiment. The doctor was anxious about certain test results: the sonograms were blurry, the images fuzzy, contradictory, the encephalograms preposterous — any diagnosis was out of the question. Every morning, he expected to find the boy or the girl dead, their burst brains oozing through their eyes, ears, nose, or throat. What bothered him most was the silence of the little lambs; they should have been chattering away by now, and he suspected that Madeleine had been hearing imaginary voices.

o   o   o

In the seventh month, a further miracle was wrought; the thirtieth and final volume of the *Universal Encyclopedia* had just passed wholesale into the ears of the little nippers when, in broad daylight and in the presence of Dr. Fontane and his sister, Martha, a babbling rose like collywobbles from Madeleine's belly: "What about the supplemental volumes? Don't forget the supplements!"

Madeleine stopped breathing. "Doctor, did you hear that?"

"Yes, Madeleine, you too?"

"Of course she heard. After all, it's me speaking," the voice went on. "Well, I'm waiting for your answer. Where are the supplements, the appendixes, the elucidations?"

"We haven't forgotten, my child. We'll get to it right now."

"Hurry up, or we'll soon be suffering from a serious deficiency."

"Which are you? Louis or Céline? The boy or the girl?"

But the voice hushed up as if it thought the question indiscreet.

"Oh, Madeleine," Fontane crowed, "it's wonderful! They're talking! We've succeeded!"

Martha, the physician, and the young mom kept hugging and kissing in a medley of laughter and tears, and if they could have they would gladly have shaken the hands of the two scamps. Instead they affectionately patted Madeleine's abdomen, trying to grab the mighty mites as if trying to catch two balloons inside a bag.

Common sense, however, absolutely required that mum be the word, at least until birth. And the team, thickening its plot, swore not to breathe a word. The hospital was already rife with gossip and the nurses were whispering about bizarre goings-on in Madame Kremer's room. The computer permanently wired to her belly was not one of the usual things prescribed for expectant mothers. Oswald, showing up daily and as uxorious as a fiancé, was unfazed by the computer. On the other hand, when Madeleine's parents saw her all abristle with tubes and drains, they sensed that something was awry, and they glared suspiciously at the cardiac monitors and the multiple crackling screens. Fontane took them aside, inundated them with techno-medical jargon more obscure than Church Latin, and had them escorted by a diligent guide who kept them aloof from any contact with the staff. Nevertheless, the team was always at the mercy of potential leaks. Madeleine was afraid that either twin might unexpectedly start talking in front of witnesses — which would have been quite puzzling. So Fontane, genius that he was, hooked up an internal telephone inside Madeleine, a very skinny wire with a double receiver in each fetus's Walkman: the wire, connected to the mother's inner ear, had a pulse ring that was audible only to the participants. All Madeleine had to do was mumble through barely stirring lips, and the children understood. It was a minor miracle of high tech, which Fontane could have marketed had he not been sworn to secrecy. Further improvements could be added later on, especially an amplifier, which would enable the babies to speak to someone on the outside without having to bawl their lungs out.

These microbes were starved for knowledge — and they were going to be served lore galore. This time Dr. Fontane, throwing caution to the wind, stuffed the machine to bursting: any dictionaries, encyclopedias, and didactic treatises sold in the finest bookstores were added to the curriculum and dished out in heaping portions to the little buggers. In less than thirty days they swallowed the latest editions of the *Encyclopaedia Britannica*, the *Encyclopedia Americana*, the *Brockhaus Enzyklopädie*, the *Oxford English Dictionary*, and the small and large *Larousse*. Furthermore, they listened to Berlitz tapes in four languages — English, Spanish, Russian, German — with which their mother had already familiarized them, and they also absorbed *Who's Who*, not to mention *The Guinness Book of World Records*. The physician, reaching into his own pockets, hired extra employees, who scoured libraries and cultural centers, unearthing rare editions and xeroxing entire tomes. Outflanked by the twins' gluttony, Fontane negotiated with data banks so he could plug into other terminals and link up with more richly supplied networks. The hard drive was already on the verge of saturation and should have been replaced by another, especially since a virus could turn everything topsy-turvy.

Monopolized by this drudgery, Fontane neglected his other patients and forsook his office. In order to cover the expenses of the enterprise, he mortgaged his condo. His aghast sister threatened to stop collaborating with him if he kept running through their joint inheritance. But Fontane, banking on imminent celebrity, never allowed himself a minute's repose. His feverish gape terrified his near and dear. Starting tomorrow, he would ignore his promise to Madeleine and begin treating other pregnant women, vulgarizing his method by applying it to hundreds of specimens. This would enable him to form an elite corps of babies who, after seeing the light of day, would always outshine their contemporaries from birth on — and radiantly at that. Instead of attending a day care center, the Fontane sucklings (that would be their name) would head straight for the university, with their little schoolbags tucked into their strollers. By the age of three they would be holding responsible positions in the business world, and every boardroom would include one or two high chairs plus a bib and rubber nipples.

o   o   o

Louis and Céline were just two scraps of humanity measuring a few scant centimeters, but they were already emitting sounds. Fraternal, or dizygotic, twins, from separate eggs and with distinct though confluent placentas, they faced each other, so to speak, but each in his or her own bubble. Their prematurity had forced their organs into place more rapidly than occurs in normal embryos. Imagine that as of the third week they were producing their own blood and had already developed retinas and spinal ganglions. They were terribly precocious, and their eyes were unsealed almost immediately. Despite the darkness, they saw each other and bowed very deeply, as befits people of the same stock. Louis ascertained that his sister's belly did not terminate in exactly the same way as his. Céline noticed that her brother had something between his legs that she did not have. They were tactful enough to say nothing: one doesn't dwell on such details. Having learned their own names from their mom, they introduced themselves to each other, and after some chitchat about the weather and the temperature, they decided to break down the partition separating them and to throw in together. Contrary to other children, they learned how to speak almost instantly. Not for them the babbling, the onomatopoeias that boggle grownups; instead they enunciated lovely, flowing sentences in a polished diction. They immediately knew how to place the subject before the verb, to conjugate all tenses, including the past perfect, and to mind their p's and q's. Granted, for a while they kept stumbling over certain mannered terms, but they preserved a well-marked taste for rare or precious vocables.

Barring instances of absolute necessity, they conversed

only with each other. Nor did they lack for topics: barely conceived, they were already acquainted with the great achievements of world civilization! Forget about calculus, the square of the hypotenuse, and the folds of the Cretaceous — *amuse-gueules* meant for nursery simpletons, which the duo had gobbled up in no time. The most intricate materials were delicacies that they hungrily chowed down on. Less than three months after their creation, they already knew about Saint Augustine: not only the church father, author of *The Confessions* and *The City of God*, but also, and above all, the very famous metro station in Paris. They could categorize gourds, pumpkins, and squashes in the Cucurbitaceae family and they knew every last detail of the polemics between gradualists and catastrophists over the disappearance of the dinosaurs. Finally, in regard to the fundamental question, "What is Mickey Mouse's name in Italian?" they unfalteringly answered: "Topolino!"

They likewise mastered anatomy before they had any, they could distinguish between the dermis and epidermis while their skin was barely delineated, and they were able to describe the genesis of the iris, the cornea, and the crystalline lens before they could even see. Unlike the common run of fetuses, they refused to be distracted by the construction of their legs and arms or the slow formation of their respiratory and sensory systems. They had an instant command of symbols and abstractions; in the incoherent mass of elements delivered to them, they effortlessly managed to separate essentials from accessories. Their improbable intelligence quotient, which no one so much as tried to calculate, helped them to solve the most intricate of problems. Nothing was so hermetic that they could not illuminate it; their mental effort ran at cruising speed. They had no time for naps: a higher mission awaited them. By the crack of dawn, when most solid citizens were still snoring away, the twins were already cramming like mad, and with every passing day they gained a few months over other babies.

The duo never lapsed into those squabbles that tear siblings apart. And if ever Louis was tempted to pinch his sister or trip her up, she gravely admonished, "No, Louis, we have more important things to do than repeat the moronic rivalries between the sexes. We ought to join forces and not hamper one another unproductively. Normalcy is not our fatherland."

"You're right, Céline! How silly of me to fall into the collective rut!"

From the very outset, they knew they were destined for an unparalleled future: chance had given them an unbelievable head start over their contemporaries, and they must do nothing to ruin this opportunity. Didn't they have more memories at six months than a centenarian? Wouldn't they soon possess the complete memory of the entire human race? Since they were already hearing in stereo and completing the development of their binocular vision, they launched into a systematic investigation of information. The only things they liked were those that challenged their understanding and titillated their intelligence. They were neither rogues, rowdies, nor snickerers; no toys or trinkets for them — theorems or theories, nothing more. They were a studious pair, always on the go. And every evening, curled up together like two reptiles, they made each other recite their lessons. The slightest lapse in the delivery of data threw them into the wildest fits of anger, and it was only because the knowledge injections abruptly dried up during the third month that the twins had finally piped up in the first place.

To tell the truth, these two human hypotheses were very reluctant to speak to their mother. Sensing that she was gossipy and long-winded, they feared getting sucked into stupefying tittle-tattle with her. They saw themselves not as extensions of the maternal body, but as two distinct individuals temporarily inhabiting the womb while waiting for the moment of delivery. They were not like those hypersensitive babies who droop or take offense when Mommy neglects them. On the contrary, all they asked of her was a benevolent neutrality. Above all, if she had nothing essential to say, then let her hold her tongue! In fact, she set their teeth on edge whenever she reread aloud some article that they had already processed and that she stumbled through like a dunce. As for the man who was seconding her, the twins were unable to picture him for now and so they merely thumbed their noses (which, appropriately, were very tiny). They had no interest in the human rabble.

On the other hand, they required Madeleine's services in order to learn how to read. Like those rustics endowed with phenomenal memories who have never opened a book in their lives, the embryos were purely the products of oral instruction. Dr. Fontane invented a system that was both tactile and visual for introducing them to the alphabet. By means of a probe, he insufflated luminous letters into the amnions, and thanks to oscillating needles the floating characters could transmit their shapes to the fingers that touched them. These palpable ABCs would dissolve within twenty-four hours. Madeleine, following the operation on a monitor linked to a camera pointing at her belly, pronounced each letter or group of letters that the twins were clutching. Able to differentiate between vowels and consonants, upper- and lowercase, they learned how to read within a week, and next, this time on their own, they assimilated the Cyrillic, Hebrew, Sanskrit, and Arabic alphabets at one fell swoop.

It was soon obvious that Céline was more than a sister and classmate to Louis: she was also a guide, who taught him about life. If she preferred the sciences while he showed a keen inclination for the humanities, her mind was nevertheless so alert and broadened so quickly that she excelled in all disciplines. She was passionate about geology and nuclear chemistry as well as the literature and great music that her mother broadcast to them through Walkmans every evening. Céline could explain the foundations of neuroendocrinology to Louis, recite a poem by Ronsard, and recognize a Brahms trio or hum the opening measures of a Shostakovich symphony, all in one breath. She was a walking — or rather resting — encyclopedia! She ceaselessly told her brother about how they had been conceived, dwelling on the sacrifice of three hundred million sperm cells so that just one could reach the ovum after an arduous voyage.

"Doesn't that prove, my dear Louis, the pitiless discrimination to which nature resorts in order to construct the finest of the finest? Bear in mind that we are the survivors of a massacre, for you and I were the only ones worthy of living."

She asked him not to worry about the vastness of his

brain, which was spilling out on all sides of his head like the outlines of a huge hat. Let the vulgar be concerned with shadow over substance. For Louis, the goal should be mind over matter: mind had to conquer matter and develop it without a fuss.

"You're not going to wax rapturous, are you, little brother, just because you're made up of water, gas, and molecules? Just because you have a rapid heartbeat and because you secrete testosterone and I estrogen? You are not going to pay any attention to the fact that I'm a girl and you're a boy, are you?"

"Certainly not, Céline. Those gender distinctions are absolutely irrelevant for us. We're way beyond the discord between the sexes."

She told Louis to feel no gratitude toward their parents: "Should one thank a man and a woman for having a good time, with no thought of us? A father and mother are merely stepping-stones for taking flight." Above all, she instilled in her twin a sense of his rank. She kept reiterating how incomparable the two of them were and how stunned the universe would be on the day of their birth. They had now and henceforth escaped the double curse that strikes mortals in their mental development: extreme specialization and thinly spread dilettantism. They would shine in every area, welding the genius of analysis to the genius of synthesis, embracing both the details and the totality. The exploration of their brains would constitute the major adventure of their lives. They would turn that dark continent into a crystalline diamond, extending their consciousness to the darkest nooks and crannies of their psyches. In short, they would form a mutual admiration society, each twin marveling at the other's sagacity. However, Céline was incontestably in charge.

Louis bowed to his sister's crushing supremacy; he was somewhat overwhelmed by how easily she grasped and retained everything. He deduced that once she was born, she would effortlessly outsail him. Not only that, but she could dance! How and when she had learned remained a mystery. Nevertheless, she taught Louis the basic steps of the waltz, the rumba, and the jitterbug. Even though the placental fluid interfered with their twists and turns, they managed to twirl like two supple fish. Seeking to relax after their heavy labor, they often plunged into a frenzied rock 'n' roll, and by the end of his gestation Louis could do up to twenty-nine different steps, including the famous move in which the man pulls his partner in between his legs and throws her over his shoulders. Nevertheless, the boy's temperament was such that he preferred speculation to parties. He loved nothing so much as studying the genesis and evolution of the great systems of thought. He already revealed a boundless attraction to G. W. F. Hegel: the German philosopher was like a spiritual brother who had been born before him and was inviting him to a colloquy across the centuries. Louis regretted that he had no direct access to the great texts. What wouldn't he have given to read, pen in hand, *The Phenomenology of the Mind*, in the original and in the various translations in order to compare them!

So now the twins decided to take their education into their own hands: they had been held back by too many mistakes. A harebrained secretary recorded the latest Sears

Roebuck catalog on diskettes as well as the 1987 railroad timetables for the Brittany-Anjou region. The absentmindedness of another secretary forced them to absorb various how-to brochures: *How to Overcome Shyness, How to Prepare Lean Cuisine for Business Luncheons, How to Avoid Dishpan Hands.* To prevent any more such blunders, the tots now telephoned for works that they wished to study. They gave their mother a spectacular bibliography, checking off the most urgent titles. It took Madeleine a long time to respond. The transmission delays in the hard drive kept growing and growing, and the narrow confines of the twins' lodging prevented any direct delivery of volumes, even miniaturized, whether via the gullet or along any other route.

By now they were fed up with being squeezed into their amnions like two dolls. They were sick of that Dr. Fontane, who spied on them, auscultated them, and breathed down their necks with fetoscopes, endoscopes, and scanners! Enough already with photos, cameras, ultrasounds, and optical fibers. Have some respect for privacy, if you please! Mom's belly was not a glass house. Dammit all, they had the right to be left alone, like any other citizen! It was time they escaped. Couldn't they be spared this burden of gestation, even if it meant putting up with a low birth weight? Would Madeleine be so good as to let them leave or would they have to beat their own path to the exit? Now was the time to see the light of day, roll up their sleeves (if that could be said of a baby), and get down to work!

Two

~

TO BE OR NOT TO BE BORN

At the start of the eighth month, Louis and Céline, out of curiosity, asked for newspapers. Clippings from the principal dailies round the world were read aloud to them. Believing someone was pulling their legs, they demanded real newspapers. Madeleine and Fontane sent them other journals. The twins were even more flabbergasted. So far, their only knowledge of the world had come from books. Everything was filtered down to them through the maternal eiderdown; events were muffled by the ramparts of the abdominal cavity. Their history lessons had taught them about battles and cataclysms, but in the haven of their bubble the worst disasters seemed no less unlikely than the most distant galaxies.

All at once they saw the light. From the first page of a gazette to the last there was nothing but stories about crimes, wars, famines, and assassinations. Could this be an exceptional day? No, the next day was the same; each morning brought the reader his ration of infamy. So this was the universe that would welcome them: chaos and terror. Not to mention the threats of nuclear and bacteriological holocaust, pollution, and galloping deforestation. In their dismay, the twins stopped learning; they removed their Walkmans, canceled their subscriptions, and refused to be disturbed for any reason whatsoever. Fontane and Madeleine were not upset. They were used to those mood swings in the twins — a little genius has a disposition of his own. But Louis and Céline couldn't get over the shock: the dreadful truth had dawned on them as they were gearing up to leap out into the world. Life would not be only a victory march; it would also be a road lined with adversity and decay. They shuddered at the mere thought of the perils lying in wait for them.

Louis was the first to come right out with it: what if they didn't leave?

"We'll stay with Mom. We won't run useless risks. Nothing can hurt us here."

"But Louis, no one can stay in a womb beyond nine months. . . ."

"We'll manage!"

Céline pointed out the difficulties confronting them: suffocation, starvation. They would grow so big that their mother would explode. But Louis dug in his heels. The more his sister argued, the harder he stuck to his guns. It was out of the question — he wouldn't insert even a fingertip into that vale of tears.

"I don't care for the life they're offering me. It really doesn't tempt me. Let's not make a fuss! Imagine: eighty billion people were born before us! What banality! Everything has already occurred: why start from scratch? Our future will be nothing but a rehash of the past, time boiled over, worn out — everything that comes to us will bear the stamp of earlier societies and centuries. No, it would be better to put off our moving day. Next year, perhaps, if the situation improves. You only get one life to live? Then I'll keep it for myself!"

Céline wouldn't hear of it. Horrified as she was by the newspaper stories, she had resigned herself to being born. She was too ambitious to stay cooped up in the uterine hideout. So many basic questions were begging for elucidation. For example, what was there before the first instant of the universe, and how could the theory of relativity be reconciled with quantum mechanics? All such questions required a team, cooperation, material, money, laboratories. If she wanted to make a name for herself, to gain even the tiniest smidgen of glory, she would have to be born.

"And frankly," she admitted to Louis, "I'm a little hot in here. It's always so moist — we're soaking in a climate of perpetual monsoons. I need coldness in order to think: no more of this dependent and overprotected pinchbeck life."

So to satisfy her lofty ambitions, she decided to take the great leap forward. And Louis, desperate not to remain alone, begged her, though in vain, not to poke her nose outdoors.

o   o   o

The great day was approaching. Madeleine, Dr. Fontane, and his assistants had absolutely no inkling of the anxieties suffered by the small uterine nation. They were preparing for the twins' arrival the way a country prepares for its national holiday. The physician had already invited a small number of bigwigs to this unprecedented accouchement. The time of secrecy was over; they could now make the matter public and reap the fruits of their labor. This would be a feat, an exploit as grand as that of the first men on the moon. Madeleine was bursting at the seams, dying to reveal her stratagem to her husband and her parents. They were certain to forgive her when they saw the results. And Oswald could have mental calculation contests with the cherubs.

Her joy was tempered by a phone call from Louis.

"Hello, darling, how do you feel?"

"Fine, thank you. We have to talk."

"What do you want to tell me, darling?"

"First of all, stop calling me 'darling'! Leave that vocabulary to dressmakers and doting puppy owners. I have to announce some news that will doubtlessly cause you distress."

"What's wrong, my little Louis? Did you have a fight with your sister?"

"Mom, Céline and I never quarrel. On principle. You ought to have realized that long ago. But I have to warn you about something: I will never be born."

Madeleine tittered melodiously.

"Don't be silly. What are you telling me?"

"The truth, Mama. I refuse to be born because the world is bad — very bad — and life is ugly and odious. I'm very sorry, but that's the way it is."

36

"You're exaggerating. Life is not so unpleasant. It has its good moments!"

"A person has to be somewhat blind to flaunt such optimism!"

"Not at all, I assure you."

"Give me some reasons to be born."

Madeleine, who had always taken refuge in a fortress of rites and habits, was stopped short.

"Well, um, I don't know — for instance, eating three meals a day, taking a nice shower, going to bed . . ."

"Flimsy propaganda. Imagine lauding sleep to someone who dreads being born!"

"There are other pleasures, my pet, lots of them."

"For pity's sake and for the last time, stop calling me your 'pet'! I'm Louis, goddamit, not your sweety pie or your honey pie or your cutey pie or the apple pie of your eye in the sky!"

"Okay, Louis, I'm sorry. You're so bristly today!"

"I'm not bristly, I'm precise! Fine, let's continue our discussion. I admit that there are those moments of pleasure, as you say, but at how painful a price?"

"You're talking like an old man and you haven't even been born yet. You know nothing. Just experience life and then you'll have the right to pass judgment."

"Mama, you wanted to teach me all about life very early on. So don't be surprised by my lucidity. In regard to the disorder of the universe, I know of only one remedy: abstention."

"My boy, would you please stop being so infantile!"

"Get a load of her! Asking a fetus not to be infantile . . ."

"You're no longer an infant."

"You mean I'm not yet an infant!"

Madeleine was climbing the walls.

"Stop playing with words. Just tell yourself that you have no choice. Put yourself in the bail-out position and wait for our instructions."

"What do you mean I have no choice? Mom, it's choice and freedom that distinguish a human being from an animal. That's been affirmed by all the good authors — Rousseau, Kant, Hegel. The first freedom of an individual is to say no!"

"Oh, leave me alone with your great writers! Does your sister know of your caprice?"

"Don't worry. Céline is willing to be born. She is totally oblivious."

"Let me speak to her."

They now had a three-way hookup.

"Céline, please tell your brother to come out. We haven't gone to such great expense just to have him mess up everything because of some weird brainstorm."

"I know, Mama, but Louis is a diehard."

"Drag him along when you come out."

"I've already tried, but nothing can get him to budge."

"Force him, show him who's boss."

"Mama, I know of no other 'boss' than authority based on persuasion. I will never coerce my brother into acting against his will."

"My decision," Louis cut in, "is nonnegotiable. Living means surviving from the very first breath; it means dying a

38

bit at every instant. I refuse to get involved in this count-down."

"Don't start again," Madeleine scolded. "I was born and it didn't kill me. And it didn't kill your father either."

"It doesn't hurt to wait. No, after pondering the matter very carefully, I refuse to be born. Besides, who's going to notice my absence? According to statistics, a baby is born every half second. So — win a few, lose a few!"

"That's not the problem," Madeleine flared up. "You were conceived in order to be born, whether you like it or not. If you don't come out under your own steam, we'll grab you by the seat of your pants."

"Mom, this conversation is degenerating, and I find it deplorable. You are no longer being guided by reason — you are now dominated by hysterics. Under the circumstances, I find it impossible to continue our dialogue."

And Louis slammed down the phone.

Up above, Madeleine, outraged by the tot's recalcitrance, blubbered her eyes out in Dr. Fontane's arms as she detailed Louis's arguments. She had recognized in him the same fear that had been paralyzing her since earliest youth. The cha-grined doctor did his best to raise her spirits, assuring her that the rebellion of one of the subjects would in no way compromise the success of their project.

"You know, Madeleine, physiologically there is nothing Louis can do. He can slam on the brakes as hard as he likes, but when the waters burst, he'll be propelled toward us — he'll be literally pushed out, expelled. At worst, we'll give him a sedative and do a C-section. If he stays inside you, he'll be in a state of sensory deprivation the moment his brain needs stimuli in order to complete its development. Believe me, there has never been and there will never be a child that remains inside its mother beyond the deadline. It's not worth antagonizing him or arousing his distrust. Let him stew in his own juice."

Louis, embittered by his conversation with Madeleine, wouldn't back down. How passionately he now hated life! He smelled pus and carrion in our finest achievements. Oh, the obscene presence of our bodily holes, exuding nonstop, leaving trails of their ooze. Human beings trickle all over; no matter how squeaky-clean a person may be, the reek of its function always sticks to a cleansed organ. And the older you get, the more your organism betrays you, relaxing its control, multiplying its involuntary outpourings. When you're afflicted by stomachaches, when a turd splits your gut, forcing itself on you like an almighty monarch, then the cloaca rises back to the surface, splattering the soul. We leak through our orifices: the nose runs, the mouth drools, the eyes tear, the ears secrete wax, and the anal sphincter is always on the verge of a débâcle. Joyfully quoting Céline's statement (attributed to Saint Augustine), "Inter urinam et faeces nascimur," Louis kept reiterating:

"The mind alone can transfigure the flesh. Otherwise the body is nothing but more or less damaged meat. This world is not the good world; it is a mistake of God's. *Real life lies ahead.*"

Louis asked his sister to imagine the fate lurking for them on Earth: they would advance from a suckling's dependency to an oldster's senility, with an adolescent's silliness and an adult's arrogance in between. No age would make up for another: a living person's entire evolution was marked by filth and decay. Louis was especially infuriated by babies since he was one himself. The saga of layettes and leashes, the epic of diapers and diarrhea — these were an infant's principal claims to fame.

Poor little pucks, all encumbered by their functions, reduced to the palpable thrills of retching and belching. At the mercy of a drop of milk going down the wrong way, having enemas titillate their anuses because of constipation, bawling stupidly but unable to speak, sucking anything and everything, even a thumb, even a pencil, drooling copiously, exasperating their parents, wet nurses, neighbors, who dream of strangling them, being born a blue baby or with cyanosis, passing from the heat of the womb to the icy cold, sleeping badly, throwing up, bathing in their excrement; and far worse, risking chicken pox and tapeworms, whooping cough and flat feet, not to mention the ickiest thing of all: the wet smooches of an aunt or grandma. And all for what? To get chowed down by rats or chewed up by a mastiff or done in by a slap from Mom when she's at the end of her tether. Thanks but no thanks! Life is a rip-off! How could billions of people have been taken in, and still no end in sight? Mankind should commit mass suicide out of horror at its situation! Do you believe that a single baby would agree to be born if it were exposed to what lay in store for it? Louis preferred to give up anything rather than pay such an exorbitant price!

Céline, as we have said, endorsed him only half-heartedly. She could already picture herself sitting at a desk, checking through specialized journals, poring over a fragment of iridium, her genius confounding the greatest scientists of her time. She couldn't understand her brother's compulsive need to fixate on details, to focus on minor miseries. "A person must be solid," she told him. "He must harden his soul, become like steel, be a block of metal, twist life the way one curls a reed. Obstacles do not diminish our freedom, they condition it." Falling back on a famous philosopher, she added sententiously: "You belong to the world that you have constructed yourself, not the world that others have built for you."

Louis admired his sister's courage and her noble adages. Yet a secret voice kept telling him to pay her no heed. He didn't give a damn about looking like a jerk. No effort of her will could change the course of things: birth is the first victory of death.

o o o

Finally, the hour of separation struck. Neither pleas nor prayers could move the little girl. For several days now, violent contractions had been shaking the habitat of the twins. Yanked and jolted every which way, they were unable to concentrate. They both realized that the great moment had come. Louis and Céline bid each other tearful farewells: entwined day and night for nine months while discovering the world of civilization — that creates a bond. They agreed to stay in touch. As soon as she exited, Céline would buy a cordless telephone or a shortwave radio to communicate with him. Furthermore, she did not despair of talking her brother into emerging someday; she would help him to take his first steps toward the light and to skirt the major pitfalls.

"Adieu, Louis," said Céline, "I'm taking the risk of living."

"Adieu, little sister. Take good care of yourself. Come back if fate is cruel to you. And above all, don't forget: we are two masterpieces."

Then a dreadful tempest swept them up, and the cervix opened, giving them free passage. They were torn away and propelled toward a narrow tunnel. On the verge of being carried off into the torment, Céline had a fit of shyness: "I can't shoot out stark naked like this, I have to cover myself." She yelled, but her cries were lost in the watery brouhaha that cascaded toward the outside. For an instant, Louis very nearly followed her, but then he changed his mind. He had taken all necessary measures to escape this misfortune: with his placenta dragging behind him like a parachute, he grabbed the cornu of his mother's uterus and, dangling in space, he let the flood surge by. Madeleine, in the throes of delivery, barely felt this additional travail. Céline slowly twisted her way through the maternal chimney, her skull squashed by that narrow casing. She felt sick to her stomach and kept swallowing all sorts of viscous stuff.

"A fine kickoff!" she thought to herself. This must be what they call the trauma of birth. Good God, what state was she going to show up in? No one would take her seriously. She should have requested a green card to work in the United States, first recruiting her main collaborators in utero. All these procedures would be a drain on her time. She should also order unlimited travel on all the airlines. So as not to forget, she tied a knot in her umbilical cord. Absolutely intent on boggling the minds of her contemporaries, she kept rehearsing the lesson that she would yell at the top of her little lungs as soon as she was home free:

"$(a + b)^2 = a^2 + b^2 + 2ab$!"

Then she instantly launched into:

"$-1 - \text{cosine } x = x^2/2$ in the vicinity of zero."

And, while the nurse would be gently cleaning her in warm water, Céline would engage the onlookers in a discussion of the logarithmic and exponential functions. She would swig champagne with the company, for she expected a small celebration on her arrival, and then she would buckle down to work at the crack of dawn. Hopefully they had thought of building small telephones proportionate to her size! Suddenly, as a ray of light filtered in, her mind drew a blank: she couldn't remember Gödel's first theorem. She couldn't have forgotten it this fast; she mustn't spoil her entrance! C'mon, let's get it together, the first theorem of . . . now whose? . . . The first what, the, the . . .

o o o

Outside, in the delivery room, a huge audience, half serious, half skeptical, was drumming its fingers. Fontane had invited all the hospital pundits, all the neonatology bigwigs, as well as medical journalists and a video team. He had lured this fine crowd by announcing the simultaneous births of a new Aristotle and a new Einstein — no less. Mr. and Mrs. Barthelemy and their son-in-law Oswald Kremer were also in attendance, the former highly reproachful, the latter slightly vexed but utterly excited about sharing his passion for numbers with the tots. He had already reckoned the exact weights of Louis and Céline, taking their mother's overall mass into account (she had gained forty-five pounds). Clean-shaven, sporting a tux, balancing fine tortoiseshell glasses between his thumb and forefinger, and escorted by his sister Martha (in her Sunday best and with a damp eye), Fontane was trembling with barely contained pride. Scarcely daring to envisage the renown that would adhere to his persona, he flashed radiant smiles at everyone. All his confrères, who had poked fun at him nine months earlier, would now be fuming that they hadn't taken him seriously. He was enchanted by the mere thought of their frustration. Armed with a mike, he requested silence; after a brief explanatory speech, he accompanied the various phases of delivery with his commentary:

"And now, ladies and gentlemen, there's the head arriving; you can glimpse the tufts of hair. Buck up, Madeleine — just keep pushing. Who'll be first, the boy or the girl? It's your bet, ladies and gentlemen. The person who guesses right will be allowed to ask the child a question. No volunteers? Too bad. Well, I'll bet on the girl; we all know how curious little girls are. There we are, the skull has squeezed through. Just look at that wide, soft caul — three times the normal size. A horrible headgear, I grant you, but it's proof of a huge intellectual vitality. Here's the face, so tiny under that helmet of synapses and neurons. The torso is out now and the belly and the legs — yes, indeed, I win! It's Céline who has honored us with her appearance. Ah, the good little dear! Hold your breath, ladies and gentlemen and dear colleagues, for the awaited moment has arrived — yes, here's the miracle baby. Silence, please. Listen to this child whose intellectual level, I must remind you, is equal to that of a Ph.D. Listen carefully."

But instead of the ravishing little fairy that everyone expected, instead of the bewitching creature who was going to curtsy and then squeal, "Where is the research program on the human genome?" they discovered a dreadful, mucus-covered mite with a wrinkled face. Terrified by the noise and the light, it could only stammer:

"Arrheu, arrheu . . ."

"Arrheu, arrheu!" That's pretty good for a newborn, but it's not exactly Ph.D. level. Confused, the physician cleared his throat and resumed his discourse:

"Hello, Céline, I am Dr. Fontane. It is I who helped to instruct you in accordance with your mother. You have never seen me, but we have often chatted. Welcome to the world. Since you already know how to read, write, and count, I am going to ask you a super-easy question in front of our friends, who have come from all over specifically to see you. Céline, while the midwife is bathing you, can you explain Archimedes' principle in a few words?"

Céline, who had become oxygenated in the air and whose skin was covered with a greenish film — Céline, wrinkled, scarlet, and furry because she had been born with hair, even in her ears, was convulsively grimacing and sticking to "ar-rheu, arrheu."

"Céline, let me repeat my question. I am asking you for a brief minute of attention: explain Archimedes' principle. Concentrate."

46

"Arrheu, arrheu . . ."

"She's bashful, ladies and gentlemen, you must understand: she has never seen such a large group of people. Barely thirty minutes ago she was splashing around in her mom's belly. Who wouldn't be frightened in her place? Céline, look at me. I'm going to ask you an easier question: what is the sum of the angles of a triangle?"

"Arrheu, arrheu . . ."

"No, no, I said the sum of the angles of a triangle. No coaching, please."

"Arrheu, arrheu . . ."

"Céline, you're not giving it your all. How much is five times eight?"

"Arrheu, arrheu . . ."

"Céline, that's enough! Let's start at the beginning: two plus two equals . . .?"

"Arrheu, arrheu . . ."

"Céline, that's not funny. I repeat: two plus two equals . . . ?"

Terrified by that stentorian voice, which was amplified by the mike, Céline began squawking, while her large brain, which had had such a difficult time squeezing through, began deflating like a pierced air chamber, under the very eyes of the spectators. And in that shrinkage Dr. Fontane saw all his hopes evaporate. The little girl kept flailing and bawling, and a nurse had to take her away.

The physicians in the assembly — up in arms at having been inconvenienced for nothing — were lambasting the whole wretched masquerade. A few had stood up.

"Please keep calm, gentlemen, keep calm," Dr. Fontane

begged, mopping his forehead with a handkerchief. "It must be the postnatal shock that's paralyzed the little girl. There's no other explanation. How can we deny that this so well articulated 'arrheu, arrheu' contains the expression of an obvious meaning, a highly elaborate babble?"

He glanced at Madeleine, who with legs akimbo and in stirrups was weeping softly. Poor Madeleine: she had agreed to exhibit herself in this indelicate posture before strangers, but now her fondest hopes had been cut to the quick. She had believed that her daughter would emerge explaining the Gaussian curvature or the Kondratieff cycles, but all the mother had brought forth was a pitifully squealing idiot. Madeleine's father came over and whispered furiously in her ear:

"You're paying the piper for your dissolute life. You're making laughingstocks of us: just look what you've done to your mother. We'll settle our accounts later."

Madeleine cried even harder, shaking her head from right to left. But Dr. Fontane went on in a jittery voice:

"Ladies, gentlemen, and dear colleagues, let us forget this little incident, if you please, and let us turn to the other twin. Where is he, the little rascal? Louis, stick out the tip of your nose, so we can question you. Push, Madeleine, don't slack off, help the rapscallion to get out. He's the one who'll save the family honor, I'm sure of it. Lou-is, Lou-is, hurry, hurry, we're waiting for you."

But, through the mother's flared navel, a high-pitched voice that sounded like the gurgling of a bathtub drain cried out shrilly:

"GO FUCK YOURSELF!"

They were flabbergasted, and rightly so, that a nine-month-old fetus — and an erudite one at that — was evincing such crudeness before even passing through the gates of life. We must, alas, condemn that deplorable habit of lexicographers, whose dictionaries include all the popular invectives, profanities, and four-letter words. Louis knew these vulgarisms by heart and counted on using them. A blast of stupor hit the learned assembly, prompting several seconds of utter quiet. They thought they were hearing things.

Fontane, who had blanched, now bleated, "Louis, come on out, we have no time to waste."

The same atrociously shrill voice repeated, "I said, Go fuck yourself. I'M NOT COMING OUT!"

This time Fontane panicked: the little fucker was making good on his threat. How had he managed it? It was scientifically improbable! And now a great specialist in embryology was upbraiding Fontane:

"What kind of farce is this, Doctor? Are you trying to make fools of us?"

"You're nothing but a charlatan," shouted another.

"You'll regret this," said a third, over the other two.

And the room exploded in furious protests, larded with insults and the scraping of chairs.

"Calling us in here for a run-of-the-mill delivery!" the great specialist went on.

"At least he can talk," Fontane countered feebly. His eyes squinted sadly behind his lenses.

"Who's 'he'?"

"Louis, the little brother."

"Are you still thickening your little plot?" scolded another severe-looking personage, his neck sporting a bow tie.

"Well, who do you think was speaking?"

"A tape, an artificial voice."

"Not at all. There's no trickery. We've just been addressed by Mrs. Kremer's male baby, and that alone constitutes a miracle."

"Do you mean to tell us," a female journalist broke in, "that there's a baby ready to be born in that woman's belly who can express itself like you and me?"

"Yes, Ma'am, a baby who not only speaks our beautiful language, but who's also got a smattering of English, German, Italian, and Russian. A baby as qualified as someone with a doctorate in literature. Do you want some proof?"

Fontane, leaning close to the parturient's abdomen, asked with a cloying lilt:

"Louis, my dear, could you repeat the exclamation of impatience that you have just articulated, but this time in other languages?"

Louis, who was not only a highly cultivated person but also a bit of a ham, did not need to be asked twice:

"Why, certainly, Doctor: va far' enculo, vai tomar no cu, va a tomar por culo, leck' mich am Arsch, ái gamissou. . . ."

"Do you really have to inflict this filth on us?" a female psychologist cut in. "None of us were born yesterday. Physiologically, this is out of the question. The acquisition of language does not begin until a child reaches roughly the age of eighteen months."

"I've circumvented that law, gentlemen, thanks to my collaborators and Mrs. Kremer."

Grudgingly, for he had been saving this morsel of bravura for the end, Fontane, without going into details, devoted a few sentences to recapitulating the history of this extraordinary pregnancy. As the narrative wore on, envy, jealousy, and incredulity were written on the faces of the onlookers, who sat down again one by one. For these satraps of surgery, these popes of pediatrics and obstetrics, dreamed of nothing less than upsetting the laws of reproduction and manipulating genes and chromosomes.

"Then why isn't the male being born?" asked a neurobiologist.

"That's the rub! A month ago, Louis read his first newspapers, and then he told his mother and me that he refused to be born. He cited the evil minds of men and the ephemeral character of existence. At the time, I admit, we didn't take him very seriously."

"The little bastard!" howled a pediatrician. "Has any baby ever chosen whether or not to be born?"

"And what about his Oedipus complex?" yelped a psychoanalyst. "How is he going to achieve an Oedipal triangulation if he remains wedged inside his mother?"

o   o   o

Suddenly, all the accumulated chagrin and frustration turned against the recalcitrant peewee. He was about to be subdued, expelled from his den. The austere clinicians and grave professors metamorphosed into hunters and seekers of justice. Overwhelmed with shame, Martha tugged at her brother's sleeve, urging him to flee with her. Fontane harshly repulsed her: Louis could not hold out for long against this mass movement. With a protracted sigh, Madeleine implored him:

"Oh, let him go, let him clear out, I just can't anymore. . . ."

Sustained by their collective anger, Fontane, brandishing a megaphone, approached all the puerpera's orifices and bellowed:

"Give it up, Louis, you're surrounded — you haven't got a prayer."

The brouhaha was at its peak. The sawbones and hole probers had all leagued together; besieging the new mother, they shouted themselves hoarse:

"Come on out, you scoundrel! Show your face if you're a man!"

The eminent specialists whooped it up around the mother like Indians around a corral of covered wagons. They were going to blithely slice into her innards and yank the rebel out. Hurry — knives, forceps, anesthetic! Go to it, no mercy, and put him in handcuffs and a straitjacket to boot. Hurry — a gas tube to stupefy him! The professionals were already slipping on their masks, smocks, and rubber gloves, grabbing lancets, scalpels, whips, saws, rasps, and pliers, preparing syringes, and dosing out the anesthetic.

"Silence," cried Louis with that grinding inflection from the depths, "silence!"

He was cornered, but he decided to go for broke.

"If you try any funny stuff, I'll tear out everything within reach — do you hear me? — the way you yank out the wires on a switchboard. I'll mix up the organs, pierce the veins, open the intestines, rip out the liver."

His teensy little hands were clutching Madeleine's bladder and duodenum and one kidney and squeezing them for all they were worth. Madeleine shrieked in pain, as if a rat were chewing up her insides. The pack of butchers about to make hamburger out of her recoiled.

"Don't do — anything," she stammered. "He's going to kill me, I can feel it. He'll stop at nothing. Oh, Louis, go away, leave me alone, I beg you, clear out with all your stuff."

"Murderer, vermin!" the doctors yelled.

Their blades hissed, raring to stab that round belly. The tumult was deafening. Passersby thought a riot had broken out.

The assembly had to face the unfortunate fact: they could not compel the birth of the child without endangering the mother's life. The physicians laid down their arms and deliberated. The main thing was to gain time, catch the little shaver off guard. After consulting with his confrères, Fontane picked up the megaphone again.

"Louis, we'd like to suggest a compromise: you come out as planned, and we'll put you in an incubator to restore the conditions of comfort and warmth you had in the womb!"

"I know how much such promises are worth — bullshit, as the Americans say. Stop trying to pull a fast one, you quack! No sedatives, no psychotropics, no tranquilizers. If I feel even the slightest abnormal torpor, I'll rip everything to shreds!"

An insult is always painful to the recipient. But imagine

PASCAL BRUCKNER

being called a quack by a prenatal brat when you're a renowned specialist or the head of a clinic! Fontane translated
the general exasperation by spewing into the megaphone,
"We'll get you, you little fucker, believe me. We'll get your
ass — I'm making this a personal matter!"

"You're losing your cool, Dr. Fontane, and you're wasting
your time. Aren't you ashamed to be talking like that to a
baby? This is all very lamentable. Tell your friends to go
home. The case is closed."

"C'mon, Louis," exclaimed the psychoanalyst, who had
seized the megaphone. "Why do you refuse to be born?
Everyone before you has accepted it. And I'm certain that
most people would give their eyeteeth on the spot if they
could be reborn."

"I'm not like the others, dear Madame. People are born in
order to learn how to speak; but if you can already manage to
speak in the uterus, why bother being born?"

"Louis, for heaven's sake," she went on with a trembling
chin that heralded tears, "be born. I'll prove to you that life
is the best thing in the world."

"Leave heaven out of this discussion! You're wasting
your breath, dear Madame."

After fitfully clearing his throat once or twice, Louis
stated in a loftier tone:

"Why do I need to emulate you, you poor earthly creatures trapped in your vanities and your petty emotions? By
what right do you intend to pass judgment on my destiny?
Freely and shrewdly and with a sound mind, I reject
existence — that vulgar, glaring, noisy thing. I leave it to
you!"

The little curser's peroration tetanized the men of science: a nine-month-old fetus addressing them in polished diction, relying on rhetoric instead of an infant's cooing! It couldn't be, and yet it was — years of scientific certitude crumbled within seconds. And when Louis added, "Keep the water, I'll just use the placenta," they were dumbfounded. All at once their fury vanished. Having lost their voices from all their hollering, they chaotically, yet quietly, surged back to their respective wards. Fontane, abandoned by one and all, looked in vain for Martha; she had long since decamped in order to hide her embarrassment. Only the cameramen remained; they kept shooting without knowing what would become of their tapes. And the mother, still pregnant with one twin, was wheeled back to her room.

Three

~

THE PEDANTIC PEEWEE

After the horrible brawl, Madeleine had but one goal in mind: to dislodge Louis, that talking tumor that had outstayed its welcome and was now defiling her. Neglecting her daughter, she imposed a veritable blockade around the insurgent. She went on a hunger strike, imbibing only a bit of sugar water each day, and cut off the internal telephone. They'd see who'd be the first to throw in the towel.

But Madeleine did not reckon on the greedy little potentate's ingenuity. Since he had a lifetime lease inside Mom, he focused on transforming this humid hole into a comfortable dacha. His mother thought she could bring him to his knees? Think again! A woman's body, especially her belly, and even more so the belly of a pregnant woman, is an inexhaustible pantry. Everything is there, within reach — the belly flows with milk and honey. Mom may have stopped feeding herself, but so what: she had months of provisions in her coffers. Contemplating those ripe fruits suspended around him, that wealth of juicy grapes, those fields of algae, those tentacles swollen with blood, sweat, and tears, he was sure he would never know want. Granted, the waters had broken. But water is one thing not lacking in a mother's interior: trickles, streams, cascades pour in from every side — all you have to do is bend over to drink or bathe. And the mucosa, as iridescent as a stained glass window, endlessly distills minuscule drops resembling glass beads. Thanks to an intricate system of dams, Louis had already constructed a small, warm pool rich in vitamins and mineral salts. In case of drought, he would go dowsing for the most accessible groundwaters, tapping whatever he needed to quench his thirst.

This left only the question of space: Louis felt squashed in his lodging, hemmed in on top by the rib cage, in front by the abdominal wall, and below by the pelvis. He had, of course, retrieved the area once occupied by Céline; he had also pushed back the liver, shoved away the alimentary canal, which was collapsing on him, and thrust aside the intestines, which were still encroaching on his territory, threatening to intertwine him in their coils. But these efforts barely sufficed. While he could move about a little there was no way he could stretch his legs, much less take a morning constitutional. He would never have enough space for furniture, not even a bookcase with confetti-size books. Louis was disconsolate. Granted, his mind had amassed so much knowledge that it would take him a long time to review it all; but wisdom is conquest, not rumination and regurgitation. And what would he do without pen or paper or any possibility of communicating with others?

He no longer dragged around his navel string; he had chewed it off with one bite and carefully stowed it away. He already had real canines, big molars: everything about him was growing so fast! And so he lived off his host — or hostess, rather; at mealtimes he would move the placenta against the richly vascular uterine mucus, and the membrane would soak up substances like a sponge. These elements then condensed into small bulges and nodules, which Louis picked like blackberries or gooseberries in a garden. When he yearned for a more diverse menu, he would go directly to the source, using a procedure that Céline had taught him. After piercing a minuscule hole into the lining of his mother's stomach, he sucked out the premasticated food the way you would slurp out an egg. He especially liked beans in parsley butter, creamed spinach, fish (in sauce or grilled — ah, tuna steak with a soupçon of curry), raspberries or wild strawberries with mint leaves and a drop of lemon juice, huckleberry jam, liquid honey, *pâtes fermentées*, and everything washed down with a good glass of wine, preferably an Alsatian pinot noir, a little touraine, a burgundy, or a côtes-du-rhône (bordeaux, to Louis's great sorrow, lay heavy on his stomach, leaving him out of sorts). But alas, now that Mom was fasting, her alimentary apparatus was seething with dreadfully bitter juices, so Louis had given up on these gastronomic razzias.

To compensate, he used various scraps from the placenta to make himself a long straw that went all the way up to Madeleine's bosom, infiltrating her lactiferous glands. It would have been a shame to waste that warm, delicious beverage, so he was suckled from the inside, as it were. Chez

Mom — room and board in abundance, hot water on every floor. Unfortunately, Madeleine's crash diet dried out her milk, and one day Louis caught a glimpse of the terrible specter of penury. Very well, thought Louis, if Mom was going to starve herself to death, he would devour her insides until nothing was left of her but a skeleton picked clean.

Every evening before turning in, to avoid an unpleasant surprise, Louis attached himself like an airplane passenger fastening his safety belt. He tied himself to all available protuberances, barding himself with telephone wires, uterine fibers, and tissues tightly strung around him. If the doctors tried to pull a fast one — say, anesthetize him — they would be unable to yank him out without gutting his mother, ripping out her bowels and viscera. She was his hostage, and she would live only as long as he remained inside her.

Madeleine was asked to leave the hospital. She should come back, they said, when the kid was willing to be born. Upon returning home, she tried to get even with her son by torturing him with the vacuum cleaner: placing the end of the tube on her right side, she switched on the power, and the child was dragged violently along. Then she moved the end of the hose over the entire surface of her belly, and the child was buffeted every which way like iron filings snared by a magnet. His reaction was not long in coming: Louis managed to grab his mother's small intestine, twisting it so violently that she passed out. But Madeleine refused to call it a day. She dreamed of strapping her son to an electric chair and calming him down with a hefty charge. She swore that she would eventually break him, that she would trample the scorpion who was digging his hole in her.

Putting up a brave front with her friends and neighbors, she said, "He's been wait-listed at the day care center, so I'm holding on to him for now." No one believed her. Although Dr. Fontane kept the videocassette of the failed birth, a pirated version was circulating, and rancorous exposés of Louis's non-birth were running in the tabloids. Madeleine had just turned nineteen, but she didn't feel up to celebrating her birthday. Oswald, showering her with affection, kept shielding her from her parents. Not content with sermonizing, they now threatened to double her debt to them as punishment for not giving birth like everyone else. Oswald too was irked by Louis's resistance; he had the girl, he wanted the boy. Every morning, on all fours in front of Madeleine's belly, he admonished Louis, enjoining him to "come out, come out wherever you are," without further delay. The boy didn't bother to respond. The mother carried you, after all; she fed and sheltered you. But the father? Do a few chance drops of semen give him any rights whatsoever? The only important male participant in this affair was Dr. Fontane, and Louis would have to avoid him like the plague.

It so happened that Madeleine could no longer count on the gynecologist. The hospital dismissed him for serious misconduct and malpractice, and the county medical board suspended his license pending a decision on his case. He had to close his office and take on various ill-paid jobs in order to settle his debts. His colleagues jeered at him or gave him the cold shoulder. And, aside from his professional disgrace, he had to endure the daily jeremiads of his sister, who, between torrents of tears, beseeched him to eat humble pie and beg forgiveness from the authorities. But Fontane dug in his heels. His instincts spurred him on: for the moment he would knuckle under; but as soon as possible, he would resume his research on a vaster scale. And then he would take advantage of his position to chastise that little creep Louis, who had made him a public laughingstock. In the end Fontane would have the last laugh. Just you wait, Louis Kremer, he thought, just you wait!

o   o   o

In desperation Madeleine turned to the last resort of the have-nots of the world: she appealed directly to God, solemnly calling upon Him to come to her rescue. But the God she invoked was a melancholy one, a God who was still surviving even though everyone had thought him dead ever since a German philosopher announced His demise in the late nineteenth century. Whether or not He existed had no impact on the course of things. Most people neglected Him, and those who worshiped Him did a poor job of it. That was why for some time now God — who had addressed mankind only three times before, through Moses, Jesus, and Mohammed as His spokesmen — had been conversing more and more often with mortals in order to convince them of His reality. Thus He was responsive to Madeleine's appeal. He kept her on tenterhooks for a few days — as was only proper — and then one morning He revealed Himself to her in all His splendor. Utterly cowed, and apologizing for receiving Him in her negligé, Madeleine humbly implored

Him to intercede with her son and talk him into being born. Granted, she had committed the sin of impatience by letting him taste prematurely of the tree of knowledge; but should she have to suffer for a gesture of excessive love? Highly irritated by her tale, with which He was already familiar (for God knows everything), He promised to make an example of this swaggerer. He checked the Great Book of the World: there had been cases of stillborn fetuses, aborted children, premature births, freaks, malformations; but infants determined to remain in the womb — never. Louis was going to pay for all his flouting of Divine Law.

Preceded by flashes of lightning and rolls of thunder (He was crazy about this slightly obsolescent ceremonial), but remaining invisible (for no one can set eyes on His face without dying), God appeared to Louis in a formidable din. Louis, believing that the physicians were up to some new mischief, was so terrorized that it took him a long while to pull himself together.

"What's happening? Where's that noise coming from?"

"Naive infant, you are scared and rightly so."

"Who's talking?"

"The Eternal."

"The Eternal? You mean God?"

"Himself."

"If this is a joke, it's in poor taste."

"Do you distrust Me, you little vermin?"

"Put Yourself in my place!"

"I, the Uncreated, put Myself in the place of a creature? Are you joking?"

"Give me some proof that it's You."

"I would be Satan if I complied with your request. God has no need of proof. He is."

"Not a bad answer. But allow me to remain skeptical all the same."

Louis had been given quite a turn: barely nine months old and already visited by our Lord! He burrowed into his basement, making himself even tinier than he already was.

"To what do I owe this honor," asked Louis, "I who am nothing or almost nothing?"

"I have come to give you an order, Louis; I command you to be born and no later than now."

"So my mother sent You! I might have suspected!"

"No one has sent Me, believe it or not, because I am the origin of everything. It is I who put a bug in your mother's ear so that she would desire to speak to Me. My sole reason for being here is to tell you this: Leave!"

"With all due respect," Louis murmured, "I'd rather not."

"No one is asking about your druthers. You must bow to a rule that has regulated the life of the higher mammals since the very first day."

"The ancientness of a rule does not prove its correctness. A mistake remains a mistake even if it is repeated billions of times."

"Come now, Louis, what are you afraid of? You're going to be born in the richest part of the world, Western Europe. You belong to a middle-class family; your dad's career prospects are good if not excellent. Despite a temporary recession, the economy is in a satisfactory state, the GNP is holding steady, and inflation is under control. What more can you ask?"

"Lord, please do not entice me with gimmicks. These slim advantages prevent neither disease nor demise."

"Well, why should they? Dying is the lot to which I have assigned mankind."

"That's just it," said Louis, wagging his head as if to demonstrate his misfortune to his fellow interlocutor. "The obligation to leave at the end poops the party for me in advance."

"Doesn't the brevity of life constitute its value?"

Louis sensed a touch of irony in the question.

"On the contrary! Its fugacity disqualifies it. Something that is not destined to last is worthless. As the first human being not to be born, I may also be the first not to die. Not bad, eh?"

There was a pause. Louis wondered if God had heard his last rejoinder — he hoped that He had left. His skull was throbbing; he felt drained. But with a terrifying gravity that was more Jovian than ever, the Almighty went on:

"You can thank your lucky stars that you have the right to live before you die."

"I don't want to do either."

"Do you really know what you want?"

"Yes, I want to stay inside my mom and read. I feel free only when I'm calm and meditating. Reality is trivial once you have a library in your skull."

"Who put that rubbish in your head?"

"Reading, Lord: it has made me intolerant of everyday mediocrity!"

"The truth is that you've read too much for your age. You could easily improve your mind in the outside world."

"No, I'd waste so much time growing, eating, sleeping. I'd spread myself thin — too many things would distract me from the essentials. And then having to endure public transportation, rush hours, bad smells — thanks but no thanks! I don't want to be afflicted by existence the way others are afflicted by a goiter."

"Believe Me, Louis" — and to reinforce His words, God switched into a formidable bass voice — "believe Me, you're wrong. You will never know the sweetness of the sun on your skin, the beauty of a twilight at the seashore; and you will grow old without ever having petted a cat or inhaled the delicious fragrance of a flower."

"Bagatelles! The nuisances I'll avoid will far outweigh those trifles."

"You're wrong, and I'm speaking to you from experience. I Myself am often moved by the magnificence of a forest or the rugged majesty of a mountain range."

"Pure narcissism of a creator — a well-known phenomenon!"

"C'mon, don't play the freethinker. Anyway, you've done enough quibbling. Pack your stuff and leave. Get going, clear out immediately!"

Oh, that unendurable authoritarian tone! Halfwit though he might be, Louis was entitled to some respect!

"Did you hear what I said? Don't add more disorder to creation than there already is!"

"You're the one who wanted this disorder, Lord. It was You who allowed evil to reign on the earth in order to tempt us."

Satisfied with this diversion, the child exploded in anger,

suddenly turning into a prosecutor. He was finally confronting the author of all our miseries, and Louis was going to pull
no punches. He waved a terrifying list of human vices, a gory
carnival of abominations in the face of the Great Clockmaker.

"For pity's sake," God boomed, "I'm not going to get into
this debate with a little man of your kidney. And first of all, I
forbid you to deprecate My work or to degrade those who are
made in My image."

"There's nothing to boast about! Don't try and tell me
that the copy is as good as the original. Just what is man
really? A talking alimentary canal, a speculating bowel, a
vermin that soils everything it touches. One example among
a thousand: pick some nice old man and put him in front of a
pile of all the excrement that he's evacuated since his birth.
That should take him down a peg or two!"

"I've never seen anything like your phobia about the
body!"

"It's not my phobia that's abnormal, Lord, it's the cowardice of other people. The body is not only the poison of the
soul, it's the soul's tomb. Tell me frankly: how can You even
look at Your creation without losing heart? What got into
You? How could You make such an imperfect world?"

"Mind your own business."

"I think I know! Alas, only vanity and sadism and having
nothing better to do — that's what inspired such a heinous
crime."

"Sadism?"

"Yes, the pleasure of humiliating us, of raising Yourself by
lowering us."

"How dare you, you corpuscle, you! Do you realize you're talking to the supreme cause of all things, Him Whom millions of believers have been cogitating about for millennia?"

"Great! . . . That just proves how servile they are. The more You mortify them, the more they venerate You."

"Louis, I'm quite indifferent to whatever you think. You make wild generalizations, you talk like a simpleton. Look before you criticize."

"My mind's made up, especially about You!"

"Once and for all, I give you existence as an act of love. Take it."

"There are presents one passes up."

"You reject what My own son accepted?"

"A lot of good it did him! You couldn't even keep him from suffering and getting crucified."

God sighed, at the end of his patience. And if you're a little thing like Louis, a divine sigh knocks you over with cyclonic force. The baby was hurled down but he kept braying all the same.

"Louis, your babbling is starting to tire Me. Behave like a gentleman. Be nice to your mom: leave her. Don't abuse the laws of hospitality."

"I'm not leaving."

For an instant, a terrible instant, God was tempted to tear the brat to shreds. He could already hear the delicious sound of the killing, like the dry crunch of a trampled cockroach. But He managed to control Himself, He let His anger subside and gradually change into malignity. In a soft, staid voice, He said:

"Louis, you disgust Me!"

"Because I've got my back up and You can't stand it!"

"Louis, you're nothing but a coward, but you'll suffer just like the others, believe Me. And someday you'll die. Just like the others."

"We'll see. In any event, Céline will help me."

"Now that you mention your sister, I was going to talk to you about her."

"Why?"

"Did you notice her muteness at the moment of her birth?"

"Yes, so what?"

"What do you attribute it to?

"I don't know. A ruse? A gene?"

"My dear little boy, you are far from the truth. Your Céline, my child, is utterly feebleminded."

And God very calmly revealed to Louis that Céline's contact with the open air had destroyed her intelligence and so totally jammed her memory that she would never recover her faculties. The girl who had considered herself the equal of Einstein and Marie Curie would never rise beyond the mental level of a village idiot.

"You're lying," yelled Louis. "Céline is holding her tongue in order to conform to the practices of the world. You're lying. . . ."

But God vanished into the ether, and a profound hush settled over the maternal grotto.

o   o   o

Louis remained prostrate for a long time. He was on his own now, with no outside ally to help him. His sparse hair stood on end at the thought that had he been born he could likewise have lost in one second the benefit of months of work! He was more determined than ever to retrench into his home, as if into a fortified camp. He despised his mother all the more for letting Céline leave, and he swore he would make her pay a hundredfold for that atrocious outrage. He would teach her what labor pains were really all about! Louis was like a tenant whose water, power, and heat have been cut off by his landlord and who is preparing to barricade the front door and the windows. The tenant was defending himself and girding his loins to endure several months of siege. For starters, he grew nails, sharpening and tapering them like so many razor blades. In case of double-dealing, he would slice up Madeleine's veins and arteries in one fell swoop. He would drown her in her own blood. If only he could add an iron hook to the ends of his little hands. Lurking in his genetrix's entrails like a wild beast, he waited for confrontation, ready to pounce. Madeleine had to know that he would not shrink from killing her, for the slightest wrong. Louis was transformed into a gladiator, a soldier: maddened by suspicion, seeing nothing around him but tricks and lies, he mounted a permanent guard, scarcely catching a wink of sleep.

The tension drained him. He was only a kid, after all! His outbursts of hatred were succeeded by long periods of prostration. He had nothing to read, and his mind was drying up, exhausted as it was by long vigils and insomnia. More than once he nearly gave up, gave out. He was at the end of his rope with this constant frazzling of his nerves. Madeleine, for her part, was broken. At nineteen years of age she felt as worn out as a matron who's had ten pregnancies. Even in her wildest childhood nightmares, she would never have dreamed she could endure such an ordeal. These were her just deserts for trying to be special, and she now begged her parents for leniency. The utterly unforgiving couple ordered her not to give in to that creep and his blackmail. They threatened her with a crushing debt and horrible punishments. She waffled for a long time, torn between the demands of her genitors and the pressure from her offspring: where God had failed, how could she ever hope to succeed? At last, greatly enfeebled by her hunger strike, she yielded to her son. She grew less shocked at the thought of his sojourning in her for a few months, perhaps a few years. She would have to get accustomed to him as to a long, perhaps incurable illness.

One day, the battle-weary mother plugged in the inner telephone and buzzed him.

"Mom? So you've finally come around! I'm glad you're listening to reason. The Fontane project wasn't viable. Yes, I know about Céline. God told me everything. It wasn't very sporting of Him. I was angry at you, but there was no way you could guess that the passage to life in the air would give my sister amnesia. Believe me, Mom, I'm the best thing that's ever happened to you. Be glad I'm remaining here: I alone will make your dreams come true. We'll perform great feats together if you obey me. You're going to do exactly as I say. I'm not asking you to love me — I don't know what that

70

word means. I'm simply asking you to tolerate me. You
wanted this situation, so you'll have to endure the conse-
quences."

Madeleine bowed, repeating to Louis that she would
nevertheless be happy if he were eventually born like everyone else. She then promptly set about revictualing him with
mental and physical food. But now the child did not wish to
receive the great texts passively; he wanted to work with a
notebook, a ruler, and a pen, and have a book bag to put away
his materials. But since his cramped quarters forbade such
amenities, he had to hit on something else. He told Madeleine to dispatch Oswald to consult specialists. They didn't
have to hunt for long. Because of the nonstop growth of
Louis's renown, a microprocessor firm built for him —
gratis — the tiniest computer in the world and a printer to
match. The terminal frame was equal in size to a credit card,
its keyboard to a postage stamp, its optical pencil to a pin, its
mouse to a shirt button. Equipped with an almost inexhaustible circuitry, the entire device weighed only four hundred
grams and was inserted into Madeleine through natural passages. Dime-size CD-ROM disks holding the equivalent of
a quarter million book pages would supply a never-ending
curriculum. Naturally, this installation was hooked up to
information networks all over the planet. The manufacturer
agreed to computerize the entire contents of the Library of
Congress, the British Museum, and the Bibliothèque Na-
tionale during the next five years. A special unit would
supervise the data acquisition and the disk pressings. This
was a trailblazing high-tech exploit, for which Louis thanked
them ardently. Eager to climb on the bandwagon, a telecom-

munications company offered the baby a miniaturized telephone jack that would enable him to reach anyone without
having to pass through the maternal switchboard. The calls
would be free of charge, and he would have access to major
satellites.

Louis, delighted to be independent at last, had thoroughly transformed his cave into an office. At the age of
eleven months, he deemed himself complete and did not
aspire to any further growth. Content to live in a restricted
space, he left to others the stupid arrogance of developing
themselves and extending their bodies in order to hide the
atrophy of their gray matter. All he cared about was the
functioning of his neurotransmitters, his synapses, his nerve
circuits. Through some strange irony, a transferal of growth
took place from son to mother: within a few short weeks
Madeleine, obeying the law of physical dilation and expan-
sion, grew another six inches, attaining the height —
exceptional in her family — of six feet two, while her weight
stabilized at around three hundred thirty pounds. She was
now a giant next to her little Oswald and her parents. From
her new elevation she suddenly saw them for what they
were: brutal, avaricious, forever obsessed with some sordid
haggling or other. And her fear slipped off her like a piece of
clothing. She needed this increase in girth and stature to
provide her child with a decent place to live. She began
going out again, although she had a hard time walking, and
passersby deferentially stepped aside before her embonpoint. No one recognized the girl of yesteryear.

Unfortunately the reunion of mom and tot was nearly
botched up. One afternoon when the Kremers' door was left

open, a nurse from the Child Welfare Department burst into their home with her scale and her vaccines tucked under her arms. Taking advantage of Madeleine's nap, she tried to penetrate her headfirst, repeating, "Sorry, Ma'am, but the law's the law. Babies have to be weighed." The diligent employee, unable to make headway, was soon wedged in like a cat in a drainpipe. She kept murmuring nonstop, "I'm only doing my job, Ma'am," and struggling furiously, her legs pedaling the air. They had to call Oswald, who grabbed her feet while Louis, from the cervix, pushed on her skull with his little tootsies. This was the only time dad and son ever collaborated on anything. The wet, vexed nurse finally came unstuck, and with bumps on her head and bruises on her calves, she had the parents sign a waiver. Madeleine vowed to defend her outposts more effectively in the future; she began by locking the door whenever she took a siesta.

Assured of everyone's cooperation, Louis went back to his cherished studies, starting completely from scratch with the pre-Socratics. He would be a philosopher or nothing. Unable to stand, despite his mother's lengthening, or to hoist up his body like an antenna in order to eavesdrop on the universe, he resigned himself to sitting at his monitor. He would have loved to puff away on a cigar or cigarette — the prototypical pose of the intellectual ever since Freud. But it wasn't fair smoking up Mom! And his den had no ventilation ducts. No matter — in lieu of space, he had comfort: his room was something like a hive, a steamer cabin, or a cradle. He should have been content to live as an amiable person of independent means, the days gliding by peacefully, the curtains all drawn, while he perched on the rich earth of global thought. But this barely twenty-inch mite got it into his head that he was predestined. He didn't have the slightest doubt: the whole world existed purely to culminate in him. He had chosen as his guide the great, the sublime Hegel; Louis was certain that this philosopher had written for him, almost two centuries in advance, what he was now living. So the tot perused the Prussian's oeuvre as if it contained a prophecy that concerned him personally. "I," he said, "am the end of history. I am the lilliputian colossus of the mind." And he strutted and swaggered, and to the two categories of "in itself" and "for itself" he added "at itself." The latter, he felt convinced, was destined to have a wonderful posterity.

And so, intoxicated with his feats, the Sagacious Brownie hurled a formidable challenge at himself: he decided to read everything. Everything that had ever been printed, engraved, inscribed on stone or papyrus, from time immemorial until our day. The literatures and philosophies of the entire world. The tales and legends as well as the guides, manuals, memorandums, almanacs, catalogs, archives, and registers. To read everything and anything in order to cope with the infinite proliferation of texts and to find the *unum* beyond the *pluribus*. The tyke would devour libraries the way others rob a corpse, until he eventually became the Word made flesh. Naturally, he was still light-years away from this ideal. But you can't get very far without a great goal. He felt as voracious as an ogre — he wanted to gulp down millennia of traditions, expand the habitual limits of the human tribe. As a deserter from life, he held a major trump card over his contemporaries: he had reduced his physiological servitude to a minimum; he was not subject to the normal wear and tear on the body. As sheer consciousness depending on a living thing, he had a discrete metabolism whose exchanges with the outside world were on the cheap. His brain, however, which at seven pounds eleven ounces was heavier than a normal brain, began pointing upward, forcing him to slant his head. Having throttled all five senses, which corrupt and mislead (Eros had no finger in this pie), Louis could abandon himself entirely to the joy of cogitation and to delighting in the world, without compromising himself there. Naturally he had his little needs to satisfy; but, being modest, they melted into the grand maternal machinery.

At an age when ordinary babies purr and babble, Louis was busily cramming on the theory of atoms in Democritus and the writing of myths in Plato. Reading and thinking meant going everywhere fast, but without actually budging. In the serene void of the motherly night, he thrilled at discovering a particularly brilliant concept or line of reasoning. His fever would rise, and he achieved a kind of spiritual incandescence — tears of admiration and gratitude welled forth, and he was floored by an all-out intellectual ecstasy that resembled an epileptic seizure. On occasion he even blacked out. After such crises, he felt like dying. How can you go on living when a book has unveiled the eternal truths in their firmament? He experienced these abysmal depressions after studying Kant's *Critique of Pure Reason*, Spinoza's *Ethics*, and Nietzsche's *Zarathustra*. These blitzkriegs of genius left him panting, broken. He had to rest, like an overworked dough. He relaxed by sucking on a teat or listening to soft classical music that his mother piped into her insides. He would then tuck himself into his warm nest, and, never forgetting to attach himself, he would doze off while chewing over a thought-provoking maxim — as snug as a bug in a rug factory.

o   o   o

Louis's reputation now went beyond the national borders. Disregarding his own grievances, Dr. Fontane launched an initiative that put an end to his foul mood. He suggested that Madeleine allow the nipper to take a major oral examination at the university before an international Areopagus of philosophers. It was high time the world sized up exactly what was happening to it in the person of this prodigy. Mother and child were all for it: Louis, so plump now that the womb was bursting at the seams, was raring to be tested. Fontane took charge of organizing the meeting — backed up this time by his sister, who preferred intellectual jousts to surgical manipulations — and he became the official impresario for the Caustic Gnome.

The session began on an autumn afternoon at the university's grand amphitheater. Madeleine, lying on a bed, was bared from navel to bosom. Her well-rounded belly supported two cameras linked to a giant screen while pickups on her abdomen transmitted Louis's voice to loudspeakers. A crowd of handpicked guests, monitored by bedizened beadles, thronged into the room, while thousands of passersby lingered outside to watch the telecast of the examination. The event was aired live on every TV channel. The

76

members of the jury, a bevy of sages and VIPs, were awaiting Louis with sniggers, all set to eat him alive. To be matching wits with not even a child but a freak, a nincompoop — it would be a miracle if this poor unfortunate actually managed to articulate the first letter of the alphabet! And so they approached the contest with a bantering tone.

They started by grilling the tyke on maieutic dialectics, Cartesian doubt, Pascal's wager, the antinomies of pure reason in Kant. Louis coasted through it all, to the great astonishment of his interrogators. He could likewise explain what distinguishes the entelechy from the quiddity, the eidetic from the noumenal. He revealed the meaning of the Leibnizian question, "Why is there something rather than nothing?" and he refuted Duns Scotus's opinion that the world is good because that is how God wished it to be.

"Yes — God," Louis felt he ought to add. "I feel comfortable talking about Him. He came to ask my advice some time ago. He was not proud of Himself, believe me!"

Between disquisitions little Louis, who could not entirely escape his age, would stick his big toe into his mouth and slurp on it noisily. Imagine Heidegger sucking his thumb midlecture! Louis would coo, and his skin would crease into lovable smiles. He would have to burp now and then after talking too fast; but does one fret over a burp when tackling Hegel's calvary of the absolute mind? Or else Louis would let go and break a slight wind, an odorless zephyr that went unheard. The severe specialists and eminent auditors were stupefied. They all kept repeating, "It's incredible"; and yet they had to bow to the facts. Several experts and ushers had checked to make sure that there was no trickery invalidating

this exploit. Their reports were unambiguous: no ventrilo-
quy was involved; it was really a baby curled up in its
mother's belly, setting forth the great principles of European
philosophy!

The exercise had gone to Louis's head; not content with
his shining responses, he wanted to dazzle the audience, to
regale it with more brilliant statements. When no further
questions were put to him he continued on his own recogni-
zance, relating Hegel's true and untrue infinite to the mathematician Cantor's notion of the transfinite; he then retraced
Ernst Bloch's ontology of Not-Yet-Being (am I intrinsically
what I am or am I becoming it?) and compared it with the
Sartrean metaphysics of Being, which is what it isn't and isn't
what it is. Uniquely sensitive to the beauty of a line of
reasoning, he juggled with abstractions and entities, took
advantage of syllogisms, and hurled out fistfuls of paradoxes;
there was no hair he did not split, no nit he did not pick —
he strutted and swaggered, carpet bombing his listeners
with his pedantry. When, in conclusion, he evoked the critique that Jules-Henri Poincaré, the French mathematician,
had applied to Kant's a priori synthetic judgments, the audience rioted. The venerable scholars tearfully gave him a
standing ovation, the entire auditorium applauding the Holy
Terror for ten minutes. Everybody wanted to touch him,
congratulate him, and since Louis's screen image was blurry
(he didn't want to show his face), they begged him to stick
out at least a finger or a toe from his mother's belly so they
could have direct contact with him. Madeleine had to be
shielded from these zealots, and there were several scrim-
mages. Once calm was restored, the head of the jury, an

august oldster with white hair, was deeply moved as he asked him, dabbing his eyes with a handkerchief:

"Who are you, Louis Kremer? An angel or a demon, a genius or an impostor?"

The little mischief-maker did not wait to be coaxed. He cleared his throat, and his piercing voice began:

"Allow me to tell you, dear human brethren, that I am the fruit of a unique mutation. Even in my original cell phase, I knew exactly where I was going. Can one even maintain that I was "conceived" in the true sense of the term? I doubt it. Had I not always existed? I therefore request that you call me Louis, simply Louis, and not burden me with a family name in which I do not recognize myself. I am living proof that the fetus is not man's initial state, but his total state, after which it is all downhill. And since appearances mask the truth, I reveal this while remaining hidden myself. Birth is death. I have avoided the supreme infirmity of decline: kinda gets your goat, doesn't it?"

The little bugger was getting all hot and bothered. He puffed up his rib cage and went on a binge with his meninges:

"I am my dearest enigma to myself; I never tire of trying to solve myself. Why, I can affirm that I've come a long way, I'm fine today — to quote dear old Hegel, 'Knowledge as the self-conceiving self' — if you catch my drift. My peculiarity? I am only a brain, a gigantic intellectual apparatus. Let me remind you that my gray matter is already functioning at thirty-five percent capacity, as opposed to the usual one percent in the average person. I hope to be operating at full throttle within a year. I can already speak Greek and

Latin, Finno-Ugric, Urdu, Serbo-Croatian (with an accent, alas), French, English, German, Russian, Italian, and Spanish (Castilian, of course). You know that a newborn baby can pronounce every sound and phoneme on earth (an ability he loses upon acquiring a particular language)? Well, thanks to my mother — thanks again, Mom — I've preserved that vast sound palette intact. I effortlessly coordinate the hundred-odd muscles that govern the phonetic activities, I — "

But Louis, having shouted himself hoarse, brutally lost his voice, and he emitted nothing but inaudible squeals. The meeting was adjourned. No matter; they had gotten their money's worth: five hours of brio, cerebral storming, conceptual acrobatics — it was more than anyone could endure. In the presence of the exceptionally gifted peewee, everybody felt stupid, worthless. The noble and hoary highbrows trudged off in a desperate and woebegone state. So many years of study only to be beaten by a papoose! The press affectionately nicknamed Louis the "Ratiocinative Pygmy" — devoid of any malice whatsoever, the nickname was simply a recognition of his indubitable superiority.

He had won! Within hours, his name and his mother's were global household words. From that instant on, Madeleine saw her Louis as a new messiah — and a cut-rate one in the bargain — a messiah who did not even have to be born to assert himself. This time she was proud of being a full-term mother, and she wasn't bothered by her son's monopolizing her. To exist robotlike to serve another — wasn't that what she had always wanted? Madeleine hired a nurse for little Céline, whose silence annoyed her, and got Dr. Fontane reinstated in his profession. Under the enraptured eyes of Martha and Madeleine, the physician had an utterly cordial heart-to-heart with the admirable tyke, promising him, as in the past, not to divulge their secret. Fortified by his rehabilitation and his success, the good doctor immediately opened a genetic genius office with new assistants.

As for Louis, to call him exultant would be an understatement: he basked in absolute bliss. An outright pasha in his mucous palace, he had fits of exuberance — dancing, turning cartwheels, singing at the top of his lungs, "I've escaped the common fate." He rejoiced like the sole survivor of a fatal accident. Céline had been wrong to leave: Mom's belly was an oasis of delights, a paradisal garden. But then again, she had done the right thing: Louis would not have put up with sharing his fame. He had truly given new meaning to the phrase "I'm living with Mom and Pop." Yet he had no special ties to his mother and sought only to maintain the conditions of eternal youth. If other women wanted to room and board him, he might consent. But he was afraid of being cast into the open air during the decanting. He trusted no human being further than he could throw him: the vile populace would never forgive him for being different. And, still fearing some treachery, he remained wary even in his most intense bursts of merriment.

For he despised earthlings, enslaved as they were by their sleazy appetites, and he wished them every possible harm. Each morning he would welcome the bad news in the press: earthquakes, epidemics, massacres, putsches, tortures — he was enchanted with these horrors. Laughing his head off, he would shout, "Great, great! That'll teach 'em!"

And he dreamed that a cosmic catastrophe would sweep away, at one fell swoop, all the rogues and wretches pullulating on the surface of the globe. What happiness he would feel by contrast, in his cocoon; how delicious it was to splash about in the primal soup! Inside his mother's navel he had made a teensy opening the size of a nail head, which enabled him to peer out at the world; if Madeleine went for a walk, he would often observe the other babies being pushed in their strollers and carriages. And upon seeing those brats — those snotnoses drooling, wailing, bawling — he would think to himself, "Oh, those assholes!"

Part Two

Four

~

STORMY WEATHER IN THE CRADLES

After his viva voce at the Sorbonne, Louis very swiftly acquired the aura of people who've fallen out with others. A single person cuts himself off, and everybody's upset. This atom of flesh, this peewee, this tiny comma in the vast text of the universe, triggered a revolution unlike any other. The suburb where the Kremers lived was mobbed by crowds of people asking for an interview, for advice. Madeleine received visitors in a small boudoir hung with pink like a bonbonnière. Reclining in a canopy bed, she was draped in a long tunic splotched with cherubs and putti. A horn, with one end hidden under her tunic, emerged from her belly like an ear trumpet; the visitors spoke their questions into the bell while Louis replied from the far end. For reasons of status this archaic system was preferred over more modern ones: you do not converse with a genius by telephone or walkie-talkie. The protocol, enforced by a master-at-arms, granted each visitor only a few minutes. The fact that the child was concealed behind his skin screen added to his spell. As placid as a water lily in its pond, Louis slurred everything he said, to the great puzzlement of his adorers. A superior mind does not speak in a run-of-the-mill fashion: ambiguity is the hallmark of words that endure.

The first disciples came pouring in, and they were able to make themselves indispensable. They were headed by a young illuminato named Damien Machereau, who had received his revelation while listening to Louis on the radio: this ex-chauffeur, a lanky guy with yellow hair and a flat, monotonous face, was a functional illiterate. Thoroughly uneducated and ignorant, he felt a boundless devotion to and admiration for someone who knew everything without ever having set foot in a school. On his first contact with the little doll, Damien discovered his own knack for stupefying persuasiveness and relentless delight in intrigue. He and his German wife, Ulrika, took over the reins of the household, asking no salary other than permission to be there.

Louis did not get any more attractive physically. Since his fontanel had never closed, his brain kept growing upward anarchically, like a sugarloaf, like a geyser of neurons twisting aloft. His head, with frontal lobes jutting out and hemispheres pouring off each side of the brain pan, had become an enormous extremity on his teensy-weensy body. Given his protruding vertebrae, his diaphanous and somewhat rubbery skin, his googly eyes, his two or three hairs like a chimney sweep's flue brush, Louis could never have claimed the title of Casanova of the cradles. Why should he care? He was pure consciousness. Nothing for appearance, everything for reflection. Besides, his deformity (which could be vaguely discerned in his always blurry portraits) was reassuring: an athlete of the cortex does not have the bearing of a matinee idol. Louis was a little monster with a simpatico ugliness.

Mineral water companies, dairy food makers, and clothing manufacturers tried to buy him with phenomenal contracts. Laboratories offered to cultivate his blood, his skin, his cells or infuse his brain in order to prepare a decoction for sluggards and goldbricks. Louis declined: he was not for sale like a vulgar soccer player! More serious, however, was that researchers hoping to penetrate his secret had attempted to bribe Madeleine and Dr. Fontane. Louis, trusting the physician only moderately, had him watched by the most ardent of his disciples — the aforementioned Damien — and that was how the quondam driver began to exert his hold over the tyke.

However, the Thinking Mosquito's intransigence was rewarded: benefactors, philanthropists, and foundations dispatched hefty checks to Oswald and Madeleine, congratulating them for having blessed our planet with this Titan of Learning. The Kremers, having suddenly hit the jackpot, bought themselves a home on the outskirts of Paris — a ten-room house in the middle of a vast park — and they paid off Madeleine's debt to her parents in full. Furious at being left out of the fun and at having no further hold on her, Madeleine's parents stewed in their permanently bitter juice. But who, amid the general rejoicing, paid them any heed?

o   o   o

Thus Fortune smiled on Louis. He now became a sort of lookout on the parapet of the human conscience, a gadfly stinging and harassing his contemporaries. He very quickly had both adulators and detractors. A darling of the media, a Pythian consulted about anything and everything, he graciously went along with what he called the vanity of human affairs. Anxious to establish his status, he participated in monthly theoretical jousts with jurists and biologists, making an effort to elucidate extremely recondite problems. He was asked, "What is your rank in the chain of life: are you a promise of existence, pure virtuality, a talking embryo, a pint-size portion? How can you think all coiled up? Is there life before life? Does all human misery come from our not remaining in the mother's womb?" Each and every time, Louis impressed his questioners with the intelligence of his replies. Some of these interlocutors dared to raise objections — they quickly regretted it! Naturally this cantankerous tad, this little bigmouth proved too much for them. The squirt had a good head on his shoulders. Wherever the *pecus vulgaris* believed it had hit the rock bottom of wisdom, he delved into new perspectives and dug out dizzying new precipices.

Some people, trying to flatter him, said to Louis, "Hail to thee, person of high lineage, high pedigree."

"For pity's sake," he bellowed, "none of that! I'm not descended from anyone, I proceed only from myself."

Major philosophers of our time killed themselves after a few hours of discussion with the baby. Louis did not weep for them.

He mourned all the less as, with growing surprise, he

noted the influence of his words on the public. Whenever he expressed himself he triggered upheavals of souls, floods of chimeras. A single phrase from this spiritual agitator would plunge whole audiences into utter irrationality. His speeches were followed by a series of disturbances, which he could have instantly disavowed. But he did no such thing. Quite the contrary, he enjoyed amplifying the unrest, and the Kremer villa was soon nicknamed the Den of Din.

The Fulgurating Brat had thus become the hero of malcontents and mavericks. He counted two very distinct categories of admirers, however: those who esteemed only his praise of knowledge and those who cherished him for his rejection of life. The former, most of them infants, emulated him with a veritable bulimia for learning. In day care centers small gangs of bookworms, dragging along their buddies, were already tackling algebra, dead languages, and molecular biology with an energy that terrified their educators. They did not *like* school — no, the word is too feeble — they idolized it. The most assiduous left home and moved into classrooms, bringing along sleeping bags and toiletries. Numerous high schools and prep schools were soon occupied twenty-four hours a day, including vacations. Teachers were dethroned, driven out as incompetents by the best students, and the police actually had to expel overachievers and star pupils who had simply chained themselves to their desks or benches.

Gloriously amused, Louis urged his little fans to indulge in their excesses. He harangued them, exhorted them to make greater efforts, to apply themselves. Every evening Madeleine kept him abreast of the ups and downs of this wild passion for knowledge, and mother and son, on their respective levels, guffawed at the nonsense of the juvenile riffraff.

"Can you imagine?" she asked. "They've had to open emergency rooms in the libraries, museums, and concert halls. In the dead of night, tearful mothers and fathers, with trembling, gaping offspring all wrapped up in blankets, ring the doorbells of the Louvre, the Whitney, the Rijksmuseum and beg the guard, 'Hurry — a Rembrandt, a Van Gogh, a Picasso for the kid. Otherwise he'll suffocate!' They seat the child in a wheelchair, dash him through innumerable corridors, and park him in front of *The Night Watch*, an Auvers-sur-Oise landscape, or *The Women of Avignon*. The cadaverous brat regains his strength, his color, and exclaims, 'How beautiful it is, how beautiful it is.' Then he asks to be wheeled to the sculpture section, and there, gently sobbing, he hugs every stone statue in turn. The same thing is happening in all European and American museums — and a few cases have turned up in Egypt, India, and Japan. In most capitals, small chamber music groups known as SOS Quartets are playing in vans day and night to supply a few notes of comfort for the most hyperactive kids.

"The situation," Madeleine added, "has gotten more complicated now that the small fry are demanding physical contact with the paintings. They're not satisfied with just looking; they have to take them down, run their little fingers over them, and even lie on them and embrace them, despite the risk of damage. Some kids very simply want to touch the eternity of the artwork — and all the clasping, hugging, and rubbing is penetrating the canvases. A whole bunch of Bosches, Brueghels, Velázquezes, Goyas, and Renoirs have been augmented by extra figures in late-twentieth-century clothes — male and female bambini who can't be erased because they're so snugly intertwined with the whole piece. In fact," Madeleine pointed out, "*The Raft of the Méduse* was supposedly so weighted down by these parasites in short pants that it literally sank into the waves, and all that's left is the surf."

Damien, who had set up a whole network of informers, reported their observations to his little master:

"Wherever children look up to you, the babbling, turbulent tribes worship you like a king. Scamps in aesthetic trances brandish your portrait (veiled) and swoop down on historic monuments, which now require police protection. Brats are abandoning Mickey Mouse and Superman to discuss Epictetus and Spinoza; a juvenile publisher has put out a bowdlerized version of Hegel's *Science of Logic*; and in the biggest high schools the Latin of Cicero and the Greek of Demosthenes have replaced slang and pig Latin, and the best students refuse to converse in anything but Sanskrit or Armenian."

Louis strutted and swaggered. He was entranced by these tales of human folly. He was truly a pebble thrown into water, provoking a tempest.

Heady with his brand-new power, he decided to systematically create a shambles in his time. And so Madeleine's bedside was thronged by a different category of fanatics, who admired the way the baby had slammed the door on the universe. They brought the tot the black book of grievances against mankind, and they confided their repulsion for this base world.

Louis aggravated their distress by whispering as unctuously as a prelate, "Do you want to be perfect? Imitate me — abstain from being born!"

"It's too late, Master, it's a fait accompli."

"Too bad. Then drink the chalice to the lees."

Bit by bit a veritable existence phobia seized hold of thousands of individuals, who demanded the right not to be born, to remain in limbo. Louis, whose popularity was now at its zenith, stoked the sedition, crying, "What? Human beings are still being born? How dare they?!"

And he commanded, "Humans of all countries, disappear, there are too many of you. Stop coupling; first of all, it's disgusting, and besides it's proliferative."

To increase the confusion, he announced that he was founding an association, Fetuses Against Birth, or FAB, and he urged children to remain inside their moms until better days came along. Heeding his advice, a few pregnant women had themselves frozen with the stipulation that they shouldn't be awakened until the end of time. Louis had succeeded in imposing a certitude on his followers: "It's better not to be!" Some adults took their mothers to court for having dared to give birth to them without first asking them, pressing for damages and interest. Some women who were about to go into labor had a moment of waffling. What if the kid regretted being born and yelled, "Put me back in the hole or I'll sue!" Indeed, lots of small fry, falling prey to Louis's propaganda, did not recoil from some discreet blackmail: "I'm willing to come into the world on the condition that I'm paid to live." Lawyers, egged on by Damien, haunted maternity wards, telling the newborns about the horror of life and dangling before them the nice, tidy settlements they could win by turning against their parents.

o   o   o

Louis was a tiny buried seed that sprouts catastrophes. He should have stopped there. He fell into a round of one-upsmanship against himself that nearly spelled his doom. Every day he dispatched couriers — messengers who propagated his slogans and tossed new ferments of dissolution into the social fabric. He encouraged the worst excesses, and he generously dispensed his vitriol to the weakest individuals in order to lead them astray. He wanted to shame people for being what they are, to make them so disgusted with themselves that they would lose all mother wit. The diminutive disturber now launched a watchword that spread like wildfire: "Everybody home to Mom!" Enraged at having been born, many people gave in to a bitter, violent yearning for their prenatal state. Whatever their age or condition, they wanted to double back through the cervix, return to the uterus, get lost in the genetrix's entrails. Many a strapping fellow rang his mother's doorbell saying, "Mom, I'm back!" and then lowering his head like a charging bull as he tried to force his way into her. They just had to be seen, those big lugs, clinging to the maternal belly like bees at the entrance to a hive. The charming old ladies had no idea how they could get away from such cupidity. Every girl having a romance suspected her lover of wanting to disappear inside her. The most fidgety of all, it seems, were the Don Juans. After roaming through so many vaginas, they finally dug themselves in, overstaying their welcome. Old roués sought the odor of the placenta in the organs of their mistresses: pecking and sniffing were enough to restore the memory of the uterine nest. Louis rejoiced at these extravagances. He could imagine all mankind's generations heading back along the endless chain of evolution, a humanity pregnant with itself, facing Adam and Eve and asking them, "Well, should we cancel everything?"

Damien was the first to warn Louis of a possible danger: the turbulence provoked by his calls for rebellion was escalating ominously. The Wondrous Triton, engrossed in his vendetta against humans, turned a deaf ear. He sneered at the rabble, young and not so young, for stooping to such a degree of nothingness.

"You're going to learn," he said, "what a little rogue like me can pull off. . . ."

Delegations of desperate adults visited the child to inform him of their frustrations.

"Master, we tried to get back into our mothers. It didn't work."

"And why not?"

"We've grown and they've shrunk. There's no room."

"What a bunch of incompetents you are!"

"What can we do, Master? For pity's sake, help us!"

"Fine, I'll give you one last chance: if you can't regress to being embryos, then you'll have to become babies again!"

Hundreds of men and women promptly obeyed this fiat.

They got together after work in bibs, Pampers, and layettes, sucking their thumbs, babbling, crawling on all fours, and getting their tushies dusted with talcum powder. The wet nurse profession went through the roof: buxom matrons swollen with milk plus soup, cocoa, beer, and wine spent eight hours a day catering to clients hanging on their every breast. It was not so much the liquid these clients desired as the sucking; they wanted to fill up on childhood. Only a small fraction of the populace was involved in these bizarre doings, but no one was left intact.

The uterine madness knew no limits. This time Madeleine, Damien, and Ulrika begged Louis to get out while the getting was good. Hostile rumors were circulating about him — he was credited with having an unbelievable occult power.

"You've poked enough fun at them," said Damien, "let them be!"

"No! There's no punishment dire enough for the crime of existing. And besides, why deprive myself of an innocent distraction if they swallow everything I tell them?"

Damien tried a different approach. He finally came up with an argument that hit home: "Don't you see that all those lost sheep are stealing your thunder?"

"You really think so?"

"And how! They're vulgarizing you and eventually they're going to eclipse you altogether."

Brought sharply to his senses, Louis realized he was wrecking his image, and he timidly backed off. Too late: by now he had launched a movement that he no longer controlled. Thousands of horrors, thousands of aberrations were being perpetrated in his name. The teensy good-for-nothing had unwittingly become the federator of all derangements. And these insanities seemed like domestic quarrels compared with what might still lie ahead. For instance: An Italian firm was hoping to launch a fad selling extra-flat embryos (a.k.a. pancake fetuses) that could be blown up with air and blood at birth for coquettes who did not wish to ruin their bodies. A few couples, citing Louis, boasted of practicing temporary interruption of pregnancy (a mother carries her child for three months, then places the embryo in cold storage, then takes it back — an ideal remedy for the lazy and the impulsive). But the breaking point was reached when even animals — no doubt contaminated by their owners — refused to give birth, and species exchanged roles: a dog pupped kittens, a cow calved a pony, a mare foaled a calf, and, even worse, after some dark crossbreeding a marecow farrowdropped kitpuppies!

o   o   o

Now the authorities, who were caught unawares for a long time (these things had been going on for almost two years), reacted brutally. They legislated obligatory ignorance for all kids under the age of six; children had to be parked in front of the boob tube for six hours each day and were not permitted to shift their eyes from the screen. To prevent the peewees from gratifying any stray impulse for culture or reading, books were put under lock and key and alphabets and primers impounded. As a precaution the government created a corps of inspectors who guarded the orifices of pregnant or birthing women to thwart any infiltration by marauders. Because fetuses had practically gone on a birth strike, government-supported laboratories worked out a new birthing method known as "Uncontrollable Laughter": the future newborn was tickled by means of minuscule electrodes until, unable to stand the hilarity any longer, he would make a dash for the outside. This was a precious advantage for nervous parents. Next — partly to calm the winds of lunacy that were sweeping through the country — the powers that be used all means necessary to throttle any attempts at second childhood. Bibs and diapers, leading-strings and rubber teats could be purchased only upon presentation of an identity card. (This right expired after four years.) Rejuvenation was also outlawed: everyone had to knuckle under to the inexorable law of time. Circles around eyes were highly favored, and heaven help the person who failed to develop another wrinkle in the course of a year: a hefty injection whitened his mane within days and seamed his face like an old parchment. Anyone caught sucking a thumb would have it cut off after three warnings.

For any disorder there has to be a cause, and naturally the rulers blamed Louis, his mother, and their devotees. The tide had turned against the Miniature Anchorite — after adulation came outrage, and he was treated like a swollen prostate, a glandular secretion. Ah, how his ears tingled! He had to break off his studies and, from his dark den, undertake his own defense; luckily he was assisted by Damien, whose maneuvering skills were astounding. Louis's fraternal association, Fetuses Against Birth, was disbanded and replaced by the Union of Babies Happy to Widen the Family

Circle or UBHWFC (pronounced "Oobhwifk"). But his tardy retractions did not ensure clemency for Louis, and for weeks on end the Delicious Chickpea expected to be torn from his downy basket at any moment and publicly pilloried. The vox populi was demanding a culprit. And once again it was Damien who came to the rescue, by suggesting a name: Fontane.

A superficial kiss-and-make-up had not dissipated the mental reservations that the baby and the physician felt toward one another. Both of them vociferously claimed credit for the same achievement: the creation of Louis. The doctor maintained that he was responsible for everything. The child asserted that he had conceived himself by sheer effort of will and that he was therefore the cause of himself. Fontane was furious — he threatened to squeal, to spill the beans. The rancor between him and the tyke boiled over. The gynecologist, who was working on an apparatus for bombarding embryos with cognitive neutrons, stated that he was close to inscribing blocks of "no-wait" knowledge directly on the brains of zygotes. Hundreds of couples had already placed orders for the procedure. There was no time to lose. In a spectacular about-face, Louis publicly named the doctor as the chief perpetrator of the chaos — the man who now wanted to mass-produce lots of little Louis clones. The tot barked out the same accusation on all radio stations, in all the organs of the press:

"That sleazy individual, under the pretense of caring for my mother, introduced toxic substances into her body and against her will, and those substances deformed the innocent lamb that I was."

Madeleine, who automatically sided with her son, confirmed his charges. And Louis hit on a formula that definitively brought him universal good will: "Prior to the right to be a genius, a child has the right to be a child."

Dumbfounded by so much ingratitude, and ignoring his sister's advice, Fontane committed the blunder of reacting with a provocation. Losing all sense of proportion, this courteous and reserved man launched into supercilious declarations:

"I could create thousands of Louis clones if I wanted to, and of a far superior quality, at that."

That was precisely the misstep the government was waiting for: Fontane was arrested, tried, and convicted. His genetic genius laboratory was shut down, his files were destroyed, and his collaborators were given various sentences. Martha narrowly escaped prosecution for complicity, and it was only the prospect of her daily torrents of tears that kept her from being indicted. But the world breathed easier: the perpetrator was finally locked away. So long as the Enlightened Suckling remained one of a kind and promised to make no waves, he would be tolerated and even welcomed — he was a symbol to all the world's frustrated.

Humiliated by having to draw in his horns and publicly admit that he was not his own creator, Louis indulged in a little self-criticism. What was his fault? He had lacked ambition, or, rather, his ambitions had been purely temporal: he had wanted to punish society — that is, reform it. What a mistake!

"Why hate people?" Damien remarked. "It's better to pity them!"

It now dawned on the child that he had never had but one enemy — God, in person — and that the real original sin was creation itself. He therefore went back to his initial project, though he modified it: his fate was to read everything, but his goal was to cure man of the illness of existence. God created the universe with one word? Then Louis would wipe it out with one word. This magic vocable, to be unearthed by dint of patient investigation, would suddenly reveal the Ultimate Principle to him. He gave himself five years to locate it and he stated the rule that would guide him henceforth:

"Laugh, human beings — dance, drink, love: I alone will liberate you from the scourge of life. I alone will drudge so that you will never have to work again. I promise you a perpetual summer vacation, peace of mind, happiness without stress."

Enigmatic as it was, this program was welcomed with respectful admiration. It looked serious, and people had the time to wait and see. The craze over the Extralucid Troglodyte was rekindled: everyone was electrified by the idea that he might soon be reading at computer speed. New believers came pouring in. With Louis's consent, Damien and his spouse officially created the Church of the Divine Child ("The child is divine because he hasn't been born"). And certain that he would write the final chapter of history, that he would be the grain of sand that would tilt the globe off its axis, the Exquisite Aphid hurled himself into his labors. Well-wishers transferred hundreds of titles to diskettes, and he enjoyed exceptional study conditions. His garret of mucus now resembled the instrument panel in a jet cockpit: several monitors, a video screen, earphones, dozens of flashing signal lights, a computer terminal, an ultrasophisticated radiophone, and a fax machine situated him at the center of a gigantic communications network, an immense nervous system that linked him to the four corners of the world. And this cobweb nourished his brain intensively.

There was no book so forbidding that Louis did not joyfully leap into it, and even the most barren volume managed to delight him. After all, books suffer from not being read — and not just books, but also drafts, diaries, medical prescriptions, promotional brochures, and even the contents of wastepaper baskets! Nothing could quench his thirst; it was a monstrous but necessary overload. Yes, for the sake of mortals — shrouded as they were in their dense darkness — he was willing to unremittingly forge ahead into the very humblest of written testimony. He had no choice: through him humanity was beginning its long march toward transfiguration.

And ignoring the slickery of cities and countries and the confrontations between races and ethnic groups, he cloistered himself in his hermitage, allowing himself only a few hours a day for sleeping, eating, and relaxing. His empire was limited to a quadrilateral the size of a page. The computer screen was his altar and his temple. Once a month he lubricated his brain by imbibing a fatty fluid donated by a neurobiology team at the University of Houston, Texas. Rocked by his mother's supple ambling in the evening, when she indulged in a bit of happy fiddle-faddling around her home, Louis was overjoyed. His cell was a blessed isle in a stupid century, and his memory a vault in which thousands of dead people were already sleeping before the entire planet would be engulfed. And everyone waited for the moment when Louis, after digesting the millions of volumes that make up the sum total of all knowledge, would in and of himself be the living Word — and a single vocable, just one, would make the solar system vanish into thin air.

Five

THE CERBERUS OF CONJUGAL LIFE

There was at least one person who was not amused: Oswald Kremer, the father of Louis and Céline. He had been hiding the truth from himself for a long time, but denial was no longer possible. His home was going to rack and ruin. Madeleine, who had never been affectionate, neglected him, fully devoted as she was to the messiah incubating in her womb. Since the money she received for Louis was more than Oswald earned, their sole remaining bond — a financial one — was broken. Louis's followers confined Mr. Kremer to a secluded room on the top floor of the villa, and they kept him discreetly hidden away. Served by a domestic, he ate his meals alone in his room; he wandered through the vast dwelling like a mobile piece of furniture. As for the child — if the word was applicable to this creature — Oswald preferred not to think of him: Louis, unwilling to receive him on the spur of the moment, gave him appointments like anyone else, and he used the polite form of address with him, pretending not to know who the man was. And little Céline, still stunted and retarded, was more of a burden than a joy.

Oswald unloaded his malaise on his parents-in-law, who lent him a sympathetic ear. André and Adelaide Barthelemy likewise despised Louis: he had never taken the trouble to speak to them and had even sent them a note saying they had no right to make any demands on him. They were terrified by Madeleine's gigantism — how could she have gained all that weight? There was sorcery involved, some magical practice that was concealed from them. Not to mention her distaste for money, which wounded them more deeply than anything else. Every time they requested yet another payment for the costs of her education, she would have an accountant promptly send them the cash without asking for documentation. They had hoped she would invite them to share her home so that they might keep an eye on the administration of her holdings — they would have been happy with an attic room, a mansard. But she had preferred opening her doors to strangers. During the turmoil that had shaken up the country, they had fervently prayed for the conviction of the Oddball Megalomaniac and had even unobtrusively joined a hate campaign against him. They would not have been displeased by a sound thrashing for both mother and child. The little creep had escaped the full brunt of the law by the skin of his teeth. At the mere thought that a whippersnapper could exert so much power, André, the grandfather, choked with anger and pounded his fist on the table.

For all these reasons the Barthelemys grew closer to their son-in-law, even though they considered him a big marshmallow. They also wrote to Dr. Fontane in prison, and putting their grievances on the back burner, they assured him of their support. A coalition of outcasts was formed, the common denominator being their antipathy to Louis. However, their interests were too divergent for the alliance to endure. Oswald, burying himself in his work as a refuge from his anguish, had begun a task that would keep him busy for many years: listing all the phenomena that could ever have occurred. Every human action is surrounded by an aura indicating all the actions that were omitted in order to carry out that single one: the thwarted vocation that you renounced, the barely flunked exam that pushed your life in a different direction, the woman you didn't have the nerve to speak to, the pin that passed within a millimeter of your eye — so many eventualities which Oswald meant to calculate as sharply as he could. Just take one year in this century and, next to the known events, picture what might have happened if things had taken a different turn. The possible and the otherwise are more interesting than the actual in its gross blatancy: they conceal better things that life has not delivered. What would have been the course of history if Mohammed had been born before Jesus Christ, if Napoleon had died in his cradle? Oswald chose to be the chronicler of hypotheses, the man in charge of unfulfillment. He hoped that by drawing up a roster of possibilities — comparable to Mendeleyev's periodic table — he could distinguish probable reality from potential and virtual reality. And he quite naturally got to wondering what might have happened if Louis had been a normal son, frail and vulnerable.

Oswald's in-laws, waving off this preoccupation as an

escape, kept reminding him of his role as father and husband. At one point, when Oswald was informing them of his plan to write the praises of the number 11, the perfect double that when added to itself produces nothing but doubles — 22, 33, 44, 55, etc. — André Barthelemy harshly cut him off: "Enough already with this mania for counting!" He was really getting off too easy, he explained. Oswald was head of his family, goddamit! Did he find it normal for Madeleine to handle such large sums and never check with him? And besides (André asked him privately, eye to eye), was he performing his conjugal duties regularly? Oswald was forced to shake his head. Was he unhappy about it? Not especially. That was a mistake. How long had it been since he had last visited Madeleine? A very long time. How long? A very, very long time. In that case, the father-in-law retorted, this was the first thing he had to impose. "How frequently?" asked Oswald. "As frequently as you like, but at least once a week. And several times a day if the mood strikes you." Granted, Madeleine was quite strong, but it was the principle of the thing. "My dear Oswald, go to your wife, my daughter, on the double and demand your due."

Oswald did not have the nerve to tell his father-in-law how scared he too was of Madeleine. Now taller than he and wider, she was no longer a woman; she was really a sea monster, attached to the human realm only by the eyes, which were lost in the puffiness of the cheeks. Horrified, Oswald forced himself to find this titanic entity desirable. Not only did he require endurance to scale this matrimonial monument, but he also feared that his little machine wouldn't size up. In order to tackle this ordeal with the greatest chance of success, he spent several weeks working out: dumbbells, jogging, biking, protein drinks. Each evening he measured the swelling of his biceps and his thighs, down to the exact millimeter. Although he put off the moment of truth and indulged in some extra days of training, he finally had to brace himself and, goaded by his father-in-law, head for the nuptial chamber. He timidly tapped on the door, requesting permission to enter in order to ask Madeleine a mathematical conundrum. (This was their last remaining form of togetherness.)

"If an eighty-year-old man has experienced three billion heartbeats in the course of his life, a number exactly equal to the elevation of a freight train on Mont Blanc, please calculate the weight of each car and the width of the wheels."

With a calm shrug Madeleine continued to leaf through a magazine, waiting for Oswald to supply the answer, as usual.

Oswald, dismayed by the immensity of his mission, dreamed of skedaddling on the spot. What he glimpsed through a gap in Madeleine's nightgown made him shudder: those trenchlike weals in the thighs, that postulated backside with its crater depths, that cascade of spare tires — he was terrified of everything about that queen of lard and pork rinds. He would never pull it off; she would suffocate him in her rotundities, drown him in her gulfs. But he had sworn an oath: he had to face the music. As oblivious as a foot soldier hurling himself into enemy lines, Oswald closed his eyes and screwed up enough courage to sit on the bed. Madeleine, taken aback, frowned and resumed her reading. With mounting boldness, he placed one hand on her fleshy wrist. It took her awhile to catch his drift. What, he had the

intention . . . after three years? Was that it? Oswald acquiesced, more dead than alive. She was on the verge of teaching him some manners by kicking him out; then, eyeing this
mannikin, who clung to her like a drowning man, she felt
sorry for him. Fine, why not do him this favor? Adelaide, her
mother, had often told her that the male animal, forever
clogged, needs a regular lube job. So Madeleine consented,
but with one stipulation: they would do nothing until Louis
fell asleep — toward midnight, as was his wont.

That same night, a few hours later, with the lights
switched off for modesty's sake, Madeleine presented herself broadside to her husband, any other position being
impracticable. Trembling, scared of being snapped up, Oswald staved off his fear by frantically calculating the weight
of his wife's skeleton, the percentage of water in her organs,
the total surface area of her epidermis (roughly equivalent to
the carpeting in a three-room apartment). By some miracle,
his little male mechanism was not a washout. Darkness had
restored Oswald's valor. He even thought, "If I were to join
Louis, his mother is spacious enough to shelter both of
us. . . ." Indeed, clasping this Himalaya was simpler than he
had thought; and it resembled the rare embraces of days
gone by. Madeleine remained passive. It was only Oswald's
humility that had allowed her to put up with a custom she
disapproved of. His reproductive organ, once so aggressive,
now seemed reasonable in size. She even caught herself
feeling a bit of pleasure and a thrill or two. She promised her
husband that he could come back every week when their
son was resting. Flabbergasted at having stormed this position so easily, the happy husband hurried to announce the

news to the Barthelemys. The reception was cool: "Come now! There's nothing exceptional about a husband honoring his duty!" His in-laws wanted concrete results, not bulletins on breeding. But in private they rubbed their hands with glee: this was a first step. The reconquest of their daughter had begun through the agency of this good soul. Ultimately they planned to do no less than eliminate Damien and his gang of morons. And so, worried lest their son-in-law throw in the towel, André and Adelaide called him every morning, inciting him to bravery, ordering him to satisfy his every last whim with Madeleine. He was the boss, for heaven's sake!

o   o   o

It took Louis a long time to notice his parents' new relationship. Since he slept very deeply, he was not immediately disturbed. One evening, however, when he stayed up later than usual because he was absorbed in Saint Augustine's *Confessions* and could not tear himself away from this exclusive heart-to-heart between a man and his God, Louis noticed an unusual warmth plus a continuous oscillation of his abode. His mother must be exercising. He deplored the idea of such late-night workouts. At the same time, he picked up some sort of dull tapping; but just as he was about to protest, he was so overcome with fatigue that he fell asleep.

The next day, thinking he had been dreaming, he questioned his mother. She confirmed that she had done some stretching to get rid of a pain in her lumbar region. One week later Oswald, in pajamas, had just entered Madeleine's room when Louis, fascinated by his reading of Moses Maimonides and looking forward to continuing *A Guide to the Perplexed* the next day, was just about to go to bed. No sooner had he thrust his thumb into his mouth — his sole concession to his infancy — than the maternal cabin began heaving and pitching again. Goodness, did Mom still have lower-back pain? How curious, this stretching in the middle of the night. But this time he heard the echo of another voice. A doctor, perhaps? a masseur who had come to bring her relief? But why that racket reverberating throughout her body like an ax smashing into a door? This was an odd way to unwedge a nerve! Unless . . . no, it was crazy imagining anything of the sort. He listened again: the banging, more and more precise, was sharply cadenced. If these were exercises, then they were the most bizarre he could think of. Again he wanted to believe that he had heard wrong; he plugged up his ears and tried to fall asleep. He simply had no right to suspect his mother. But what about that surging, that rolling? He was enraged, furious. Could Madeleine possibly have lied to him? There were two things Louis couldn't stand: romantic passion, which darkens reason, and the unleashing of the senses, which degrades people. The commotion faded after several minutes, and Louis wondered if he had been prey to some hallucination.

Nevertheless, out of prudence he let on nothing to his mother, and noting that the same thing had happened at the same time each week, he decided to wait. The following Thursday he stayed up after switching off the lights. His worst suspicions were confirmed. Everything recommenced, and the shaking got harder, knocking him out of bed. This time the collision was serious: some not-very-nice things were happening in these caverns. The telephone receivers jumped off on their own, the computers flashed, the fax hiccuped, the radio crackled, and Louis, knocked about, felt his dinner rising to his lips. The pigs! He wanted to get to the bottom of this, so he climbed through his cabin all the way to the bottleneck that communicated with the lower stories. He wanted to perch on the fallopian tubes in order to have a front seat; but any access, aside from a small fissure, was plugged by a mucus stopper. Putting his ear to the ground like an Indian, he made out a hammering very close by: it sounded like a struggling beast trying to break through some wall, and every assault rang through Louis's skull. Banging his little fists, he shouted, "Damn it! This is an incubator and not a brothel!"

His protest was drowned out in the general brouhaha. He felt discouraged. His panic increased when his mother distinctly pronounced a name: Oswald! So the intruder who dared to stick his nose into Mom's calyx, disturbing the peace of these enchanting premises, was Oswald!

How humiliating to picture the "head of the family" perching on her like a huge drone — it broke Louis's heart. As he indignantly brooded a wild panting began, and the shock sent him sprawling against his radiophone, leaving a bump on the back of his head. He should have attached himself — his brains were being shattered because of an oversight. For several seconds an earthquake, following a release of energy inside Madeleine, turned everything topsy-turvy; then calm was restored. In his terror, Louis was about to retaliate. He changed his mind. Perhaps his mother was likewise victimized by this man, who had forced her to commit ignoble acts. Louis could have summoned Damien and his team and ordered them to punish this degenerate, lock him up and even — why not? — emasculate him. But a messiah does not request help from mere mortals, so Louis made it a point of honor to settle the matter himself.

Knowing that his genitors mated every Thursday between midnight and one A.M., Louis prepared the necessary equipment for his plan. He acted frisky and deferent toward Madeleine to avoid arousing her distrust. He was set on catching the thieves red-handed. A week later, several minutes before the appointed time (his "parents" rutted punctually), he once again suspended his research to undertake the strenuous drudgery required to carry out his plan. Having braided the umbilical cord into a solid cable, Louis now hooked it to his wrist. Everything was ready when the convulsions began. The heat mounted, the atmosphere thickened, the walls transpired, the orifices moistened, the entire lower abdomen became full-flavored. Louis was soaked. "The bastards!" he cried. "They're at it again!" He held on for dear life, awaiting the worst, and was soon buffeted by a full-scale tempest. His computers shook perilously; Louis was scared they would fall on top of him, since he did not have enough rope to belay everything. This time Madeleine's spasms were far more intense than usual. Could she possibly be feeling even the slightest pleasure?

Louis perceived some rapid seesawing just a few centimeters away: a blind brute was making its way through Madeleine's belly, rubbing against delicate fluorescences, sweeping away any obstacle in its path. To be faced with his parents' intimate secrets, his nose against the delinquent object, as it were — what a dismal situation! Poor mankind! Why must adults always turn into animals when reproducing? The huge spermatophoral pin kept charging in and out, consigned to the stupid mechanics of the male. The child, attempting by hearing alone to evaluate its caliber, had noticed that the thing stopped at regular intervals, either at Mom's edge or way down deep, where it banged away obtusely as it tried to push beyond its limits. It had to be grabbed then, when it was exhausted by its excursion — or incursion — and it was enjoying some R and R. It had to be blocked so that it wouldn't lash out. Louis had made a noose with the other end of his cord — which was as supple as a vine and as solid as a lasso — and now he slowly slipped it through the narrow passage of the cervix, as slender as the slot in a piggy bank. The loop was the exact width of Mom's tunnel and should be just right for capturing the beast that haunted it. If only Louis had a hand grenade or a stick of dynamite: he would have disabled the hideous snout within seconds. After laying his snare Louis waited, as patient as a trapper.

The temperature rose but nothing happened. Had Louis been found out? Had his father smelled a rat and given up? Then an incredibly violent tremor brutally jolted the entire region, launching a more intense bombardment. "Dad" was in rare form tonight; the affair was getting dangerous. And indeed, the flesh stake was smashing full-force into the far end of the gut. Up there, the amorous rutting reverberated once again. Nearly losing his balance, Louis just missed plunging head-first into a cavern. He had to act now, before "Dad" fired his missiles and got away: this racket signaled an imminent release. As luck would have it, the monster paused for a few seconds. A fatal blunder — it was time enough for Louis to waylay his prey; he yanked the lariat, which tightened and closed inexorably. Plunging backward, he braced himself with all his strength: if only the cord didn't break. It was a tug-of-war between the thing and Louis. From out there horrible yells, curses, and shrieks burst into his world. A panic-stricken Louis very nearly let go in order to plug his ears. He was so small, so frail!

The pressure was dreadful. His hands bled, clutching the cord, and a cramp sliced through his left arm. How awful for him, the pure elixir of cerebrality, to be reduced to a degrading fistfight with a — let us not shun the word — dickey-boy! But it was Louis's duty to pounce on Papa's peepee and tear it out of Mom's sacred vase. If he had been born, Louis would have devoted his life to extirpating lechery in every human being; he would have been a lust buster, a phallus tamer. Firmly planted on pubes and montes veneris, he would have fended off the attacks of licentious sabers, crossed swords with the attackers to bar their way. He already pictured himself as the Batman of beds and boudoirs, swooping down on eiderdowns and pajamas, coming to the rescue of virgins and wives — all of them victims of the unleashed harpoon. So many rodeos to look forward to!

Luckily, he was sustained by a saintly wrath! And his vigor was increased tenfold by the notion that in a different life he could have been the champion of abstinence, the Carry Nation of vice. He simply had to stand his ground and crush Sodom and Gomorrah once and for all! Oswald, light-years away from the truth, believed he was being held prisoner in the pincers of an enormous lobster. For all his moaning, he refused to move lest he exacerbate his pain. And Madeleine, whose tender flesh was martyrized by the cord, was suffering in the very place where she had felt a pleasant warmth just one second earlier. Ah, so much for the trumpeting and gibbering! The moment of repentance had come. Feeling he had a solid grip on his aggressor, Louis managed to disengage one hand and pick up the receiver of his telephone. As it happened, his mother had not switched off the line, and she now picked up. He triumphantly announced that he had captured that randy goat known as Oswald Kremer. And Louis would release him only if Kremer promised never to darken this door again.

"What, Louis, it's you who's — "

"Whom else did you expect?"

"I just can't believe — "

"Believe nothing! Just deliver my message."

"I'm horribly embarrassed. Here's your father: you can talk to him man to man."

Oswald, panting with pain, was floored by the news. He bawled into the receiver, "Let go of me this instant! That's an order! Your father demands it!"

"Oswald, the word 'father' has no meaning for me, and no one gives me orders!"

"If you don't obey, I'll spank the living daylights out of you!"

"A spanking? And while you're at it, why not whip me, garrote me, impale me? Ten physicians were unable to dislodge me from here, and you think you can terrorize me with the threat of a spanking? You poor runt! Now listen to me:

Mom is not a sow you can knock up, a bitch you can cover, or a flue you can scrub out. I'm involved in research that's crucial for mankind, and I won't tolerate a stranger in my fiefdom. I repeat: no hanky-panky with Mom!"

"Louis!" Oswald was beside himself. "I'll do anything I want to with your mother — she's my wife. You can be sure she agreed to it and even enjoyed it."

"Liar! I forbid you to talk like that, Dad!"

In his paroxysm of fury, the Little Angel had called him "Dad" — he was losing all self-control. Foul words gleaned from his endless reading, language we would never have dared reproduce, spurted from his lips like pus. What was that voice speaking inside him, that voice of a fishwife spewing the worst abominations? Both Madeleine and Oswald were agog, and Oswald stopped resisting.

"Okay, Louis, let me go."

But the adorable Bread Crumb, carried away by his rage, grew even bawdier in his florilegium of filth, flaunting a confounding inventiveness. And with each spurt, he further tightened the cord.

"Louis, I beg you, let me go. I'll never come back again."

"You're not getting off that easily. You're going to apologize for soiling Mom with your insinuations. Say, 'It was I who forced these disgusting things on Madeleine.' "

"Fine, it was I."

" 'And I'll never bother her again.' "

"Never again."

"Say, 'I swear'!"

"I swear."

"Louder."

"I swear, Louis, I swear."

Louis bit through the cord. Oswald pulled out of his wife's belly and gazed piteously at his appurtenance, which had been turned purple by the horrible lace. His son's nastiness had brought tears to his eyes. Madeleine, likewise sobbing, tried to console Oswald as she smeared unguents and pomades on his wounded perch. Nevertheless, terrified by the child's determination, she decided to close shop for good as far as her husband was concerned. There was no way she could go against Louis's will. Oswald had to cave in: mortified, thinking he could glimpse sly smirks on the faces of the brat's followers, he waited several days before reporting the disaster to his parents-in-law. They didn't offer a single word of compassion — they reproached him for his cowardice, and André even ventured to apply the epithet "milksop." Oswald realized that he had outstayed his welcome. He buckled: the ordeal had broken him.

o   o   o

Louis tried one more time to approach Céline, the only person he was attached to by a bit of the love and warmth that one seeks in family relations. She had not recovered her mind, and she would spend whole days prostrate in bed. Relegated with her father to the top floor of the house, she was pale and skinny, her hollow eyes as black as if they had been soaked in ink, and the only language she emitted was an occasional curt yelp. No one could understand why a little girl who had mastered the great theorems of physics in her mother's womb was now utterly unable to articulate even the most elementary syllables. Once or twice, however, she had unexpectedly spoken, repeating the same maxim in the husky voice of an old crone: "You scour cucumbers with kosher salt." Of the thousands of laws that she had learned this was all that remained — the start of a kitchen recipe! Such fits of memory had no sequelae. In time little Céline became aggressive toward other children, pouncing on them in the street and biting them or pulling their hair, so that her father had to keep her at home. She was so joyful watching parachute jumps on TV one day that Oswald gave her a domestic hot-air balloon with a *couchette* basket. Céline got into the habit of living in the air, just beneath the lofty ceiling of the earthlings who fed her through a system of pulleys. And they never got another word or another sound out of her.

All these events had a profound impact on Oswald. An orphan with nothing but vague work-related acquaintances, he gradually lost all joie de vivre. Distrusting everything, especially numbers, and suspecting only flimflam and make-believe everywhere, he stopped taking anything for granted. Eventually he even doubted his own doubt and questioned his very existence. This came almost as a relief to him: what he had thought he had experienced had never happened to him! He had been tormenting himself for nothing! Therefore he stopped eating — does one feed a ghost? — and remained in bed, silently lapsing into a state of extreme feebleness that reinforced his conviction that he was nothing. In the end he died without realizing it, without knowing he had been alive.

Oswald succeeded on at least one level: he had persuaded the others that he was nothing. His passing went unnoticed, and his corpse remained cold for over twenty-four hours before it was discovered by a servant who happened to enter the room. Madeleine, who hadn't spoken to him since that unfortunate evening, didn't bat an eyelash upon hearing the news. Needless to say, she did not attend her husband's funeral, and the undertaker's assistants had to ask the guests to shed a few tears in order to maintain a mournful atmosphere for the ceremony. Their daughter's iciness terrified Mr. and Mrs. Barthelemy: they could already see the fate in store for them when death came knocking. The horrified parents drew away from their daughter and her child, moving several hundred miles from the villa. Adelaide Barthelemy, who could not forgive herself for abandoning Oswald, was even more upset than her husband.

She got into the habit of sewing every day, tirelessly refastening the same buttons and remending new garments. Overpowered by this mania, she began sewing anything and everything: tablecloths to tables, her husband's trousers to a chair, the chair to the carpet . . . She always had a needle and thread on her and never fell asleep without a sewing kit under her pillow. Wherever she went, she would burglarize the notions shops. Her fixation led her into the countryside, where she traveled with yards of thread under her arm to sew up all the empty spaces. She couldn't stand gaps, breaches: the world was full of holes that had to be filled. She tied trees together with huge, fragile tapestries, wove mobile footbridges over streams, and indefatigably patched up the landscape. Several times state troopers, notified by farmers, had to escort her home after confiscating her materials. She also tackled living creatures, catching flies and bees, May bugs and mosquitoes and sewing their wings to their abdomens — a delicate task requiring the utmost attention and the finest of needles. She also sewed together the paws of dogs and cats, who fled her like the plague. Now and then in cafés and supermarkets she assaulted young people, wanting to sew their hair to their foreheads to keep it from fluttering in the wind. She sewed her own mouth together into a hermetic seal. Then one day a napping André caught her trying to pierce holes in his lids in order to sew up his eyes. He called the police and had her put away. Adelaide was confined to the same institution as Céline, whom Madeleine had decided to get rid of after Oswald's death. But since grandmother and granddaughter were in different wards, their paths never crossed.

When he was informed of his father's demise, Louis uttered only one word: "Finally!" Once again, Dr. Fontane, literally consumed with rancor, tried to put spokes in the tot's wheels: alerted by a letter from André Barthelemy that poignantly described Oswald's death as well as Adelaide's illness, Fontane decided to burn his final bridge. He had nothing left to lose. From the depths of his cell, and with a fierceness multiplied tenfold by his incarceration, the physician indited a pamphlet entitled *How I Manufactured Louis Kremer*. Exposing all the details of this venture, beginning with Madeleine's first visit to his office, the text reduced the enterprise to a mere combination of luck and guile. At the end of this confession, he blurted out the terrible truth — anyone can have a child on Louis Kremer's mental level: "Louis is a genius not because he is exceptional, but because he has not been born." The brochure was mailed to all the media. Damien offered to take out a contract on the prisoner and seize hold of the organs of the press. Louis dissuaded him: Fontane's statements were so gross that no one would believe him. And indeed, no newspaper would publish the doctor's revelations, which fizzled out amid a general indifference. Fontane thought he was sowing a whirlwind, but he reaped a fiasco. And Louis rubbed the irony in by writing to the prison administration and asking for a lightening of the doctor's sentence in the name of humanity and compassion.

Having thus shunted aside all remaining nuisances, the Most Illustrious Squirt kept gaining momentum. The very next day after his father's decease, he gave a dazzling lecture at the United Nations offices in Geneva (Madeleine was flown in on a special jet). Commenting on a conundrum of Plato's — "What exists always and does not become?" — Louis replied very simply: "It is yours truly, damn it! Me, myself, and I, and not the cosmos or eternity." The females in the audience swooned before his erudition, and his squealing voice sent shivers up and down the spines of the coquettes. Oh, the dear little smartypants; oh, the itsy-bitsy darling; it was the coolest thing that ever happened to them. They did not tire of listening to him spout, though he deafened them with his gift of gab. He certainly had a head on his shoulders! What mom didn't dream of having a little domestic dragon of his stamp in her belly! And when young parents mated, they would murmur, "Make me a Louis!" Actually, the Omniscient and Omnipotent Solomon was so learned that no one could check his statements: people just listened and waxed ecstatic. From now on, even though he couldn't be seen inside his hideaway, he wore a beige silk loincloth. Occasionally he would work for such long periods, thirty-eight to forty-eight hours at a stretch, that the neurons on the top of his brain formed minuscule connections in the roof of the womb, and they took root there. Louis was planted head-up, like an upside-down tree.

Here and there small disturbances still made the headlines — secret covens of imitators of the Divine Child became more and more rampant; whole school classes played hooky to secretly comment on Homer, Milton, or Dante; newborn babies, disappointed by the state of the world, promptly headed back to Mom — but the Sublimissimo granted them neither recognition nor support. Sometimes, alas, he was tormented by horrible jokes: during radiophone conversations, uncouth callers would invite him to perform indecent acts, and viruses in his computer confronted him with distasteful messages. Louis forgave them all: he felt more pity than antipathy toward human beings, who never control the forces that dominate them. No matter what they said, no matter what they did, his spiritual grandeur rendered him inaccessible to their abuse. He would not even pay them the tribute of his anger, when with one word, just one, he could save them from the chasm of suffering and grant them eternal bliss. Mercy was his sole offense.

As he advanced in his odyssey, recapitulating literature and philosophy, he drew closer to his infinitely simple and infinitely complex formula, compared with which the Talmud, the Koran, the Bible, the Gospels, and the Vedas, in unison, would be nothing but puerile chatter. He could sense it, it was right there, within reach — it almost raised the mass of texts like a dough. To think that with the purifying puff of a word, he would be offering the Absolute to the human race — it was dizzying. In his pink flesh-cupboard, Baby would soon possess a sovereign power: the ability to dismiss this world the way you switch off a TV set. Since everything is written, it is enough to read everything. And everything will be consummated.

6

⌢

THE GARDEN OF EARTHLY
DELIGHTS

Now a long period of har-
mony commenced between Louis and his mother. For the
first time, the Brilliant Scatterbrain grew aware of the sacrifices that his presence inflicted on Madeleine. For his sake
she had renounced everything, even a human form. She had
become a pretentious hag who was so overweight that whenever she moved, the folds in her skin had to be carried like a
bridal train. Stuffed with infant meat, she existed solely as
the jewel case for the Precious Solitaire reposing in her
womb. Out of goodness and self-interest, of course, the child
decided to help her: weren't they two convicts shackled to
the same chain, tied together by a common fate?

Louis now had more time at his disposal: he had stopped
receiving people, stopped giving audiences and lectures —
he had totally isolated himself from his fellow men. Attuned
to living on heights beyond anyone else's reach, he could not
waste even a minute on exchanges or controversies. Since he

was able to overcome all eternity, why bother frittering his life away on useless quibbling? Human beings had nothing to offer: either they were in agreement with him, and so he had nothing to debate; or else they would bicker, and a word, a single word, from Louis would cut the ground from under their feet. He was tired of these facile victories over contradictors who instantly bit the dust and admitted defeat while praising him. He would jump down their throats: "Your criticism was annoying, but I find your approval even more irksome, and your kudos antagonizing." Complimenting him meant limiting him, reducing him to the size of a superlative. Never once had he found an adversary who had seriously manhandled him; their rebuttals were so poor, their defense systems so precarious! As for the great names in philosophy, none could hold a candle to his. Even Hegel, that behemoth of the mind and Louis's first idol, was no longer worthy of having the child rinse his fingers in his cephalo-spinal fluid. He was a mere freshman, a rookie, when all was said and done. Baby had no more masters of thought because he out-thought them all. In the firmament of Ideas, he was the only star that shone.

Louis had therefore assigned his disciples the task of convincing humanity and preparing it for its redemption. Louis, all by himself, constituted an army, a government, a nation. Tens of thousands of people around the globe were working for his Church, preaching the good word and aiding the Kremer house — now known as "the Castle" — by collecting hundreds upon hundreds of texts, which the little cannibal instantly devoured. Other people existed for him only as executives, as so many ears, arms, and brains that passed his orders on. The more the mob of the faithful increased, the more the transmission organs multiplied.

Relieved of all propagandizing and missionizing, Louis agreed to assist and help out his mother. A physician friend sent him a video disk containing a detailed map of the maternal abode, and the child quickly noted the overall plan. He learned how to distinguish the sense nerves from the motor nerves, and he familiarized himself with the neurovascular system as well as the ninety thousand miles of blood vessels. For starters, he devoted several hours a week to doing a little interior gardening inside Mom. He greased and lubricated her organs, and with a flick of his green thumb, he emptied cisterns filled with suspicious liquids. Armed with a swab, he cleaned the dirty viscera; he also cauterized tiny wounds, wiped out burgeoning centers of infection, and skimmed overly rich humors. Furthermore, brandishing a tiny pair of scissors, he cleared his immediate environs of underbrush, cutting off outgrowths and smoothing out puckerings. Finally, clutching a rake, he gathered the refuse and traced lovely, regular patterns on the ground. One had to see him, this knight of the ovaries, this baron of the pancreas, clearing away the bile, brushing the colon, unblocking a vein in two shakes of a lamb's tail. No surgeon was more dexterous. Louis found no task too repugnant: he was simply maintaining a machine (which just happened to be his mother), and he saw these functions purely as technical problems. Upon completing these chores, he went to splash about in his swimming pool.

Mom was a basin of cool water, a greening countryside, an

abundant orchard, a stagnant bog, a dark cellar. As a top-level employee of her internal highway department, Louis gradually became the indispensable auxiliary of her well-being. He was so intimate with the maternal landscape that he could predict anything that happened, predetect any irregularity and mount a preventive counterattack. Louis feared only one thing: that his mother might someday undergo surgery, above all in her abdomen; that criminal hands, taking advantage of the windfall, might violate the uterine sanctuary and forcibly yank him out of his refuge. By what authority could he oppose an operation if Mom were suffering from a tumor, if her state of health justified a hysterectomy, a removal of her fallopian tubes? And so each morning, more vigilant than ever, he inspected every last nook and cranny with the patience of an entomologist, tasting the blood and the oozings to locate any abnormal flavor.

Whenever Mom suffered from constipation, his little hands would squeeze the huge main sewer, the lazy cloaca, until things started moving again. Whenever Mom was fast asleep and her bladder was about to run over, Louis would sound the alarm. He didn't want water damage causing a short circuit in his computers. "Hey, up there. Wake up, please open the dikes." Whenever Mom was in a melancholy mood, with a patch of fog rising in her stomach, Louis would blow through her duodenum in order to disperse the mist, while the shreds of bitterness slipped away in colorless vapors through her mouth and nostrils. Naturally, Louis's field of action was limited to the immediate vicinity of the womb. To get at more remote places, he would massage his mother internally, reckoning on a gradual benefit for the entire organism. Thus he cleared up his hostess's migraines by accelerating the blood flow from her belly in order to help dilate the vessels in her skull. And every evening, curled up into a ball, he would roll around on the lining of the uterus to produce a strong, relaxing heat that brought comfort to Madeleine. Sometimes she dreamed that Louis was caressing her skin, leaving long, delicious traces, with a long brush as gentle as a rose petal and as raspy as a cat's tongue. Knowing how intransigent her little savior could be, she refrained from asking him for this treat.

∘   ∘   ∘

Louis was thus promoted to the rank of official guard of his mother's body; thanks to his diligent care it was in perfect health. Her faith in her son was so enormous that she entrusted him with the keys to all her apartments, even the most microscopic. Around his waist the child permanently wore a whole set of rings, pass keys, and hooks that jingled and jangled at the slightest quiver. Yet all these measures did not save Mom from a severe bout of bronchitis that dragged on for nearly a month. During that period Louis was unable to concentrate. Even in normal times Mom was the seat of a tremendous commotion, and Louis was prey to a cannonade that would have driven out even the most hardened souls: her mere blood pressure produced a continuous hum, her digestion the loud sounds of detritus, her heart the clanging of a gong. Not to mention the gas, the gargling, or, even worse, the farts that trumpeted forth, the belches that exploded in her ducts with the violence of a hurricane. But when Mom suffered from her cold, the decibels mounted alarmingly, and Louis came within a gnat's eyelash of ordering tranquilizers just like anxiety sufferers in the outside world. Mom would spit, sniff, snort, snuffle, and gag, creating a perpetual quake in the uterine lining. Her coughing spells knocked the child for a loop, forcing him to fasten his seat belt; her snorting and snuffling drilled and bored into his ears; and when she expectorated after clearing her throat, the tot, sucked upward, feared being disgorged like a vulgar blob. Ah, what a loquacious nose Madeleine had, what a chatty goglet, what a talkative siphon, what a voluble snout! In short it was a domestic hell, and neither antibiotics nor aspirins could bring the infection under control. Louis, thoroughly undone, had to face up to his powerlessness, and he would have given anything to gain access to her bronchi, her throat, or her sinuses in order to unblock the excess mucus. Eventually, after ravaging the area and spreading tears and pain, the germ gave up the ghost, and life went back to normal. But it had been a close shave!

On the whole, however, Madeleine was quite robust, aside from a little hypertension due to her obesity. She owed her constitution to her youth (she was only twenty-two) as well as her ability to sleep for weeks if not months on end. Of course, given her weight and size, numerous activities such as high-jumping, roller-blading, and trapezing were off limits. Even going out was difficult, because her legs barely supported her and she had to be moved in a wheelchair or a palanquin. So she spent most of her time lying down with her eyes shut and reaping profits from her nights. She hired herself out to overworked businessmen, students cramming for exams, lovers eager to give themselves to one another without pause. By a simple touch of her hand she absorbed their fatigue, sleeping it off to fulfill the contract. Her clients perked up and strode out smartly, even after several all-nighters. Madeleine could have written "Professional Sleeper" on her visiting card.

Congenital insomniacs, the genetically exhausted who had been sleepless for generations and whose babies came into the world with huge dark rings around their eyes, mobbed her for consultations, hoping Madeleine would wipe the slate clean of their arrears of months and years. Madeleine combined sleep periods and, in case of great demand, would doze off for forty-five days at a stretch. She had found a lucrative occupation that dovetailed nicely with her condition and added to her already abundant revenue. Everyone went to her for recuperation. Asleep, resting on plump pillows, she was the equivalent of the total population of a small town in a state of hibernation. Adding up the orders from her customers, she calculated that she was condemned to two centuries of nonstop torpor. Luckily for her, her rest had an extraordinarily restorative quality, so that a single night's sleep could satisfy the requirements of several nights for a number of clients at once.

Her own son likewise entrusted brief snoozes to her when he absolutely had to finish the complete works of some important author. Upon emerging from these reading orgies, he would swaddle himself in her like a bug in a rug, yielding to three or four days of utter sluggishness in her company. Numb with weakness, mother and child would jointly descend to the kingdom of the dead, engulfed in an

abyss of warmth and beatitude. The uterine hideaway became the land of a closed, perfect eternity. The first person
to wake up would take care of the house, barely breathing,
giving orders so that everything would be ready when the
other came back to life.

o   o   o

A small gadget, a miracle of microscopic engineering that
some physicians lent to Louis, was to confirm him in his role
of shepherd of the maternal flock. This doohickey consisted
of a pair of infrared binoculars that combined the functions
of a telescope, a magnifying glass, and a telephone: not only
could you see things near or far, but also, thanks to an
incorporated mike, you could speak to whatever the eyes
picked up. With the help of these glasses not a particle of his
mother's body would escape the tot; he could view the very
core of any object, down to the nucleus of every cell. Louis
would have much preferred being miniaturized himself,
piloting a bathyscaphe through Mom's veins, chugging
through her tracheal arteries, tobogganing through her di-
gestive tract, or, even better, becoming a speck of saliva in
her mouth, a molecule in a tear beading in the corner of her
eye. However, since science was unable to shrink a human
being to the size of a microbe or bacterium (otherwise the
whole of mankind could be contained in a single pearl),
Louis had to content himself with having only his gaze
penetrate the maternal apparatus.

Thus, sitting as a cross-legged astronomer, he would set
out daily to explore Madeleine's interior. He concentrated

right off the bat on the infinitesimal. It had the depth of a second universe; he managed to observe lymphocytes and polynuclears exchanging information, DNA filaments stretching out, and even atoms measuring only several angstroms (one ten-millionth of a millimeter) dancing in a Brownian motion. Whenever he zeroed in on a particular point he would send out a beam of rays, and the pencil of light would arouse an entire buried world that coiled up on its secrets the way an oyster shrinks back from the tang of a lemon. Louis was ecstatic about how clean and tidy these domains were: Mom was truly a Swiss on the inside, an impeccable Helvetian housewife. In the course of this excursion to the outskirts of the minuscule he discovered lands uncharted by medicine. Under Mom's impure receptacle, not far from the womb, our Proud Fellow stumbled upon a pit where strange things whimpered. Adjusting the lens to its utmost acuity and delving into that depression, he spotted a throng of tiny wiggling eels, among which our dumbfounded viewer recognized the spermatazoa previously dispatched by Oswald during one of his rare visits with Madeleine. Louis had no trouble identifying them since he had been of their number, and he felt he could make out a certain family resemblance.

What were they doing there? How had those myriad bacteriological hoboes managed to survive? Their normal life span should not have exceeded forty-eight to seventy-two hours. This herd of pariahs was emitting a collective sigh. Plugging in his receiver, Louis listened: these prostatic legions were bleating; this vermicular tribe was articulating a kind of incomplete, mutilated pidgin. Pricking up his ears,

Louis understood: since they themselves were only the fractions of human beings, they cut their words in two, usually omitting the vowels. Is it possible that the consonants form the masculine part of discourse and the vowels the feminine part? (Louis vowed to mull this hypothesis over.) He quickly figured out how to complete the abbreviated sentences, for these earthworms, chattering extempore, kept rehashing the same story: they had come within a gnat's eyelash of entering the ovum, and a fabulous destiny would have been theirs but for their rotten luck. "I," said one — and Louis restored the missing links — "I was meant to be a geometrician . . ." "And I an oyster farmer . . ." "And I a headhunter . . ." "A C.E.O. . . . ," "A fighter pilot . . ." They all indulged in the same lamentation: "Oh, the metabolic superiority of the ovum, which is ninety thousand times more voluminous than we!" A few howled in counterpoint, "We don't need an egg, we're self-sufficient!" The others resumed, "Oh but we do, oh but we do!"

Why, what was at the ends of these gametes, what was fidgeting at the tips of their flagella? Louis couldn't believe his eyes: dunce caps! They were wearing that token of infamy to expiate the dishonor of their failure. Oh, these nullities! Thus the spermatozoa, discontented with having to wallow on some biological sidetrack in a woman's belly, were already acquainted with the Darwinian principle of selection! Louis found this voluble and viscous guano repugnant! He was revolted by the thought that he came from this, that he had been part of this pullulating phratry. He could not help calling to those losers. They began seething, turning their sham heads toward his voice, trying to make contact with him. And in their amputated idiom (transcribed here into good English) they asked, "Who are you, boy? Why do you use such long sentences?" (Through living together in a hot, seminal camaraderie, they knew of no other form but the familiar.)

"I am the realized one, the accomplished me, the ace of aces. I exist only by dint of your elimination — my success is built on your disaster. And *I* am speaking normally!"

He burst out laughing. It was like pouring acid on a serious injury, and a tempest of bitter retorts whirled up from the earthworm people.

"You're lying, we don't believe you."

There were all speaking in unison.

"Sorry to disappoint you, but it's the whole truth and nothing but."

"Tell us how you pulled it off."

"It's easy: from the instant I set out, I was chosen by the ovum. A chemical emissary had secretly contacted me, saying, 'You are the most able; take your time, you will win.' If you others had known what was in store for you, you would have prudently stayed put in Papa Oswald's stables. But like helots, at the first signal from the folliculina you ducked right into the trap. No sooner did the ejaculation begin — an unpleasant moment, I agree — than I started moving up toward the fallopian tubes at regulation speed. How many of you jostled me, trying to displace me, but only to end up in some deep dungeon? I therefore passed unhampered through the cervix and blithely swam on, certain of reaching my goal. Eventually, exhausted by this odyssey without victuals, I was lucky enough to see the ovum open its barrier and instantly shut it behind me. In short, three hundred million set out, only one made it, and that was I."

Another shudder ran through the slugs. Louis, who had made sure not to mention Céline, awaited their reactions.

"Listen, what is life like up there?"

"Life is a long calvary. You can never thank me enough for having spared you."

And Louis, hoping to discourage them, painted an apocalyptic tableau of the human condition. A thousand noises emerged until a half-voice rose to present a half-request: "For pity's sake, help us to tackle the ovum again. Give us another chance."

Louis, exasperated by this deafness to his arguments, exploded: "But I tell you, you slimy earthworms, life is a prison, a horror, a baseness — you don't know how lucky you are to be here. There are no make-up classes for existence."

The mollusks refused to back down: the same request rose from their slobbery seething.

"Please help us get out of here."

Peering at these parasites with their ludicrous grace, their simpering and mincing, Louis got scared. If the semen had miraculously survived for a few months after emission, then, by some other miracle (a helping hand?), they might hoist themselves up to Madeleine's ovum and saddle her with a child. Louis had to get rid of them as fast as possible.

"Now listen up, you gang of wrigglers, in order for two or three of you to make it into the egg, they have to shove aside all the others and wipe them out. There are about two hundred million of you: 199,999,997 are outstaying their

135

welcome. Work it out among yourselves, clean up your act, and when only the best are left, I'll see what I can do."

It was a gross ploy; but no sooner had Louis spoken than the pile of maggots ferociously plunged into an internecine war, suffocating themselves in their own coils, exterminating themselves joyfully. Oh, that squalling, that slimy hecatomb! It took Louis several days to recover. To think that his mother harbored such horrors! He shivered in retrospect.

As he went on with his prospecting, he especially scrutinized Madeleine's brain, sinking deep into the immensity of that celestial vault, which was as dark and contrasty as the other. He differentiated the sites of pleasure, sympathy, and taste and plumbed the two hemispheres and their cortex. Then, in perusing the psychomotor area, he located a supernumerary ventricle from which a stream trickled as from the lips of a wound. Louis examined it for days on end, hesitated, and finally had to admit: this outflow was the very source of speech and thought in his mother! Yes, indeed, that notch, buried under the brain's convolutions, harbored the wellspring of the mind. Louis had just unearthed something that alchemists and philosophers had been vainly seeking for centuries. Like all the great explorers, he had made his discovery by accident, so he would not let it go to his head. He would be charitable: he would not insult the world's scientists by trumpeting his revelation loud and clear. He would continue to say, as the neurophysiologists believed, that thinking is not localized. No use shattering common illusions. For he owed his acumen solely to the fact that he resided inside Mom — a unique position for ferreting out the most closely guarded secrets.

Like the hevea tree, which disgorges its rubber, the ventricle in question distilled a continuous filament of vocables and phonemes, which scattered, tangled up, to irrigate the entire head. Louis noted that thought is a bleeding wound, a hemorrhage that is torrential or anemic depending on the intensity of mental activity. Thought snaps, crackles, and pops words and abstractions in a long, uninterrupted ribbon, and Louis, subdued, believed he had made the dream of all men come true: the dream of directly reading someone else's mind. Louis could almost have touched his mother's ideas, deductions, reasoning; he could almost have weighed them, disassembled them. This intellect-in-the-rough emanated a rare beauty, and when Madeleine concentrated or talked a blue streak, it was transformed into electrical energy, pouring into stars and sparks that illuminated even the parietal dome and the brow ridges.

Right underneath, vague terms, uncertain or discarded opinions, all the ordinary refuse of a reflective life dripped into a small basin from a bulge like the burner on a kerosene lamp. Sometimes this recycled magma recurred in more elaborate forms. What vitality! If a person of only average intelligence manifested such vim and vigor, then what about a da Vinci, a Mozart, a Picasso? Even the cerebral slag of those figures must have been gold nuggets compared with the discernments of your man in the street. And Louis did not dare to think of his own brain, that most complex marvel of marvels. For several days he remained dazzled by his mother's conceptual pandemonium, occasionally perceiving a fleeting scruple or a pang of conscience, or else a fine, but undeveloped, insight that perished like a shooting star in the neuronal matter. Some convictions were radioactive, emitting joy or sorrow; there were thoughts as light as teenage girls or as severe as cardinals, resplendent hopes in a succulent green, anxieties the color of anthracite, worries resembling a winding sheet. In a gelatinous purlieu far beyond the occipital lobe, Louis actually stumbled upon a small declivity where countless answers were waiting for their questions. These were simple replies for the elementary situations of life; they jumped about impatiently in their purgatory, ready to pounce on the sentence or query that would vindicate their existence. Louis very nearly asked them a question, but held back, fearing as he did a slapdash or imprecise response.

The mental fairyland inside Mom also contained more equivocal phenomena. One day some abnormal signals put Louis on the trail, in the cerebellum, of a kind of smoking volcano surrounded by a black, fetid moat. This crater was filled with sizzling verbal embers, as it were: all the insults that Madeleine had choked down, all the horrors she had imagined but not dared to articulate. A pantry of gross words and foul thoughts! Louis wondered where his mother could have learned such blasphemies — which propriety disapproves of and censure represses — those expressions that must never cross a woman's lips, especially when she's your mom. And he had not yet drained his cup of sorrows: under that burning smut another, more violent fire was smoldering, invisible to the naked eye. Louis thought he could make out sneers mingling with sobs, obscene rattles, howls of terror, ignoble imprecations. Sheltered from the flames a witches' Sabbath, a dance of monsters and chimeras, seemed to be running riot. In that mob atrocious, raucous voices were calling for someone's death, demanding the prosecution of a name — always the same, it was a name Louis thought he knew but couldn't quite catch. He was amazed that no slab sealed off that center of filth, and he didn't even dare picture what would become of Madeleine if some unfortunate eruption disgorged that garbage, mucking up her mental apparatus. All at once he felt very cold. Try as he might, he was unable to pierce the whirlwind of fumes escaping the pit or to hear any sound distinctly. Luckily a thick layer of flesh, muscle, and tissue separated him from that evil land! Ultimately he gave up: Mom had the right to her secret garden, even if it was a heap of manure. Fearing that his desire to shed light within her might create new zones of darkness, Louis abandoned his binoculars like an overworked toy.

o   o   o

It wasn't long before he succumbed to the spell of a further surprise. During that euphoric period a group of Japanese scientists, friends and admirers of the baby, offered him a holographic device that could project moving images onto the lining of the womb. This device enabled the Delectable Duckling to receive the world at home and to invalidate God's prediction that Louis would never see a sunset or a flower! Into his dwelling he invited the Alps, the ocean, the plants, the rain forests, the diverse varieties of insects; he trod on anthills, butterflies fluttered around him, a bee alighted on his nose. A bedlam of birds chirped in his domicile (the device included a sound track), pecking away in the

139

top stories of his brain, singing on his shoulders while ruffling their feathers. A cat rubbed languorously against his legs, a spaniel lay at his feet, a panther leapt upon and over him, a scorpion stung his heel. Wasn't it extraordinary to enjoy everything without touching, to be guarded in this way against contact, which soils? Every day a sumptuous menagerie filed across the walls of his cave, as if Noah were parading the occupants of his ark.

Louis juggled with the sun, saw it rise on his left in the morning and set on his right in the evening. The child turned the planets upside down, slept with the moon under his pillow, reached into the Milky Way and picked a multitude of stars, creating a luminous dust on his skin. He managed to gather a whole village and its inhabitants in the palm of one hand, while his other hand flung thunderbolts at this populace. The rain did not soak any more than the sun heated, even if the pedestrians and animals did scurry to seek shelter from the drops and the wind.

Above all, however, Louis, who had already read the equivalent of two hundred fifty thousand volumes, saw a real book for the first time, an edition princeps of Bossuet's *Sermons*, bound in cordovan with thick yellowed paper, fine typography, wide margins, and gilded capitals like keys at the start of each chapter. For days on end Louis shifted the book around and around, peering at each facet; he even thought he could smell the characteristic mustiness, like the aroma of an old vintage, and hear the noble rustling and crackling of turning pages. Trying to prolong the enchantment, he asked for a permanent projection of an illusory library around him, a mixture of classical and modern authors in all languages. Some adjustments were made, and his wish was granted: after all, what good would a technology be if it could not satisfy our most far-fetched whims?

Louis slightly relaxed his iron discipline. He got into the habit of receiving a chamber-music group once a week, and its members, wearing tuxedos or evening gowns, would perform a Mozart trio, a Bach suite, or a Brahms quintet. The child also played imaginary tennis matches with a fictive partner who lobbed the ball back with an unreal racket. Yes, indeed, after his hard labor, His Little Majesty planned to grant himself some distraction, some R and R. This was truly a happy period, and every morning Louis would thank his lucky stars that he had not been born. The world came to him spontaneously — and not in its crude materiality, but reduced to a diagram, the world as idea. Sometimes he became so joyful that he felt he was like other men and eventually considered them his equals. Yet he could be nobody's equal, because he was superior to everyone. Above all, he had no right to happiness, that intoxication of the mediocre. Saving the riffraff forbade any convenient abandon. During that period, the Little Chap was made a knight in the Legion of Honor, taken into the Order of Merit, and awarded a Purple Heart by the United States government. He was also made an honorary member of the Académie française, dubbed Lord of the Crown by the queen of England, and given honorary doctorates by a half dozen universities around the globe. Naturally, he also received the Nobel Prize, in every category. Louis thanked them: he knew that his contemporaries valued such baubles and bangles. So why slight them? He pretended to be flattered.

In the face of his exceptional intelligence, the most elementary laws of science began to wobble: there were whispers in the community of scientists that the earth might very well be flat, as Ptolemy claimed; that the sun — yes, indeed, contrary to the mendacious allegations of Copernicus — revolved around our planet, which was therefore the center of the universe; and that, finally, it was not the apple that fell to the ground, Mr. Newton, it was the ground that rose toward the tree. Louis let them talk: he was beyond such contingencies.

Glamorous beauties, actresses desired all around the globe, slipped him perfumed envelopes containing highly suggestive photos of themselves. Louis sent the pictures back without a comment: the world, yes, but not the worldly.

And now, aware of his absolute grandeur, our Small Fry, as part of his plan to refute God, decided to speak about Himself in the third person and to capitalize Himself on all occasions. This was the tiniest of details for someone preparing to inhale the great soul of the universe and dissolve it. With a termite's hunger He continued to clean out libraries, and in a single day He would integrate and digest whole spans of history. He had just learned Quechua, Samoyed, Bantu, and was about to tackle MonKhmer and Aleut. His brain, still growing and as malleable as clay, resembled a wax Tower of Babel, a cylindrical gland rising brick by brick and curving like a banana over his forehead. Whenever He meditated intensely, luminous plumicorns rose on the highest boughs of this horn of plenty, and, from a distance, He could have been mistaken for a display of fireworks. He was truly the Beacon of the Human Race.

He experienced the acme of contentment the day the National Ballet holographically performed Tchaikovsky's renowned chestnut *The Nutcracker Suite* on the palm of His hand. Louis was particularly moved by the easy motions of a ballerina named Lucia, an eighteen-year-old of Italian background. This dancer, with a sweeping curve of back and lovely chestnut curls, had green eyes speckled with gold and skin as pale as the finest paper. Carried away by her grace, He dreamed about her for several nights in a row. He was not unsettled by this blaze of dreams. He was immunized against the physical and its vile sorcery. He was heading toward the Absolute under the best of conditions, and he was already enjoying a glorious, virtually rot-proof body. Yet He suffered, knowing as he did that this poor ballerina was condemned to live out there, on the other side of the frontier: why not invite her to His Eden and spare her the normal human miseries? It was more than a good idea, it was a noble deed. And the Hermit Rascal, under the influence of a sweet intoxication, kept trying out a few dance steps, as if life were to become a long, never-ending waltz.

Part Three

Seven

〜

LOUIS THE CONCUPISCENT

A series of disruptions was to tarnish the happiness of the Cogitative Pygmy. To begin with, God abandoned mankind. He was exasperated by its intractability. He had believed that men would sing His praises for centuries upon centuries; He had seen to every last detail of their existence, even allowing them the freedom to disobey Him, to wallow in sin. But He had received no gratitude. He who knew the number of scales on every fish swimming in the seven seas, He who knew the name of every single one of His creatures as well as their phone numbers (even disconnected ones) found Himself paralyzed by their fickleness. It was no use His saying "Take infinity and eternity, add the speed of light, sprinkle in a few billion stars, and you still won't have the foggiest notion of My greatness" — humans didn't give a hoot. Whenever they raised their heads, it was not to celebrate the Almighty but to watch planes zoom by. One incident in particular had hastened God's resolve: a group of experts at the International Monetary Fund, assigned the task of calculating the cost of this planet since the Big Bang in dollars at the current exchange rate, had just issued a highly critical report. They excoriated the phenomenal waste of energy, the thousands of extinct species, the continents that had risen and then vanished, the overly numerous tongues, races, ethnic groups — not to mention the useless organs and functions of the body. Why two legs, why ten fingers and thirty-two teeth? Why so many varieties of flowers, insects, animals? And why the four seasons: would not one have been enough? It was simple: there was too much of everything — we would have to trim the fat, reduce overhead. The outlay was astronomical!

Oh, the wrath of God! He was so disgusted that He decided to chuck everything. He could have punished these mortals, destroyed their cities, unleashed the fires of heaven upon their assemblies. But He was weary both of inspiring fear and of dispensing mercy. The world deserved to be forgotten, not saved — on this score, He almost agreed with that stubborn slime Louis Kremer. Nevertheless, God did not retreat without sowing two seeds of discord: He sent a final ordeal, in the person of young Lucia, to that little pinchbeck messiah. And He notified several press agencies about His departure (the worst thing would have been for His retirement to go completely unnoticed). Stunned by His formidable absence, authorities from all religions went off the deep end. What had gotten into Him? What had people done to Him? They hastily organized prayer vigils, collective penances, public fasting. In vain. The heavens remained empty! God wasn't dead: He was gone!

148

It was at this point, quite accidentally, that a group of South American theologians traveling through Israel exhumed a very ancient Aramaic manuscript at a monastery near Jerusalem; the document, which predated the birth of Christ, announced that the Divine, prior to being the Word, had been of a musical essence. His first manifestation was a sound, whose quivering in the original ether engendered the universe. This thesis instantly made the rounds of the planet, and everyone drew the ineluctable conclusion: if God was originally of a melodic nature, then only a melody can bring Him back to us. No matter how much the priests ranted and railed that God's Word demands constraint and not seduction, and that music is too indolent, too grandiloquent an art, they nevertheless had to knuckle under. Therefore they begged the world's greatest musicians to deploy their talents and haul back Our Lord by lassoing him with a cantata, a symphony, a concerto.

The musical craze gradually infected all classes in all countries: presidents and cabinet ministers got into the habit of receiving one another with songs, and policemen were verbalizing by vocalizing. Hard-boiled lugs warbled as gracefully as castratos. Everyone tried to contribute to the cause on his own individual level, and you would have thought you were in an endless musical comedy. The slightest conversation — now hummed — sounded like a recitative. Street vendors hawked little two- or three-minute ditties aimed at Him up there. Day and night, the best singers and conductors put on unforgettable concerts that were far more magnificent, far more sumptuous than anything ever played before; the marveling listeners fell to their

PASCAL BRUCKNER

knees, weeping with joy. There was no way that God could
resist such an avalanche of splendor. "C'mon, come back —
listen to how beautiful this is!" Performers killed themselves over a squawk, an ill-timed lurch, a too-speedy tempo.
Being good meant nothing: you had to be at least excellent.
This perpetual enchantment transfigured human life: everyone preferred music to anything else, and for its sake people
began neglecting their duties as spouses, parents, citizens.
Since it was our Father who was arousing this profusion of
sublimity, a thrill of affection for Him quivered throughout
the universe.

Only atheists and free thinkers protested against this
hullabaloo. The religious fanatics, they said, were creating
generations of deafness, and for the most obscurantist goal
imaginable: to call God back to Earth! "You ought to applaud
His departure!" they said.

Louis, from the depths of His niche (don't forget that He
too had the right to capitals), Louis, who was plagued by this
craze for the divine and whose mind focused chiefly on
receiving the young ballerina, outdid the protesters:

"He's gone? Wonderful: I am here, I! He's had His time;
He's a usurper."

But no argument stopped the extremists: they needed
God on the spot, just as you might need a piece of chocolate
with your coffee. He alone guaranteed that life is not a
dream, that our senses are not being abused by a wicked
spirit. The Almighty, however, lay low. Moving Him seemed
as difficult as tickling a mountain. No matter how many big
fanatics jumped into active volcanoes in order to be propelled nearer my God to Him, He was unfazed. A disc

150

jockey in Hamburg broadcast a new idea: maybe God was fed up with masses, motets, and oratorios. What if he preferred jazz, rock, house music? What if he felt like hearing a solid jam session? Immediately, anyone that the five continents had to offer in the way of soul, rap, reggae, and pop got into the act. What a racket: discos were roofless now so He wouldn't miss a note, and sleeping became virtually impossible in the cities. Not even the countryside offered a safe retreat — the noise caught up with the most isolated hamlet. The sound tissue rising from the planet was so intense that it jolted the entire solar system; old stars fled, whole constellations tumbled from the Milky Way like rows of pearls from a necklace. This brouhaha exasperated our lower brethren, already maddened by the disappearance of the Great Clockmaker: frogs, cows, donkeys, and poultry croaked, mooed, brayed, and cackled away at the sky. The worst were the dogs: they all barked in unison. They got beaten, but they kept on; they were slaughtered, but as their souls soared toward paradise, they continued barking. Their masters, flabbergasted by this uproar, started baying themselves when their favorite animals died. They had to be muzzled. Meanwhile, musical instruments started playing all on their own, grinding out the same songs over and over. Their owners hammered them into silence; mourning the loss of their boon companions, they reconstructed them the next day, sometimes on a disproportionate scale.

Ah, they were far from the magnificent musical emanations of the beginning! The charivari grew so loud that it awakened several corpses: believing that the hour of the Parousia had struck, they rose from their graves, clutching their old skin envelopes and waiting to be adjudged a body again and endowed with the three attributes of eternity: beauty, subtlety, and impassibility. They were urged to be patient and to return underground.

Once again, madness led men astray, and Louis was alarmed: would He again be held responsible? One day a young British virtuoso, carrying a viola, climbed the Alps all by himself and mounted a platform ten thousand feet above sea level. There he tormented the strings day and night performing Bach suites, until a gust of wind blasted him into a ravine. His immolation was contagious, provoking a flat-out exodus to the peaks: people vied with one another in their dashing upward, ever upward. Entire orchestras emigrated toward the summits, which teemed and swarmed with thousands of people eager to charm their Father. Rock vocalists in boots, hats, and leotards, followed by their groupies in miniskirts or gym gear, crossed paths with men in dress coats and women in evening gowns, their beautiful hands in silk gloves. Despite their competitiveness, these musical families, assisted by porters who lugged the heavy instruments on their backs, helped one another over raging torrents and up the steepest slopes. Cable cars were mobbed by soloists in evening dress, little guitar strummers with long hair, jazz drummers raring for a good fight with the Unlimited. Neither cold nor vertigo nor the discomforts of altitude could stop them. Once perched on the crests, they pierced the air with deafening adagios; they sent almost unbearably intense sounds from valley to valley. The men and women way down on the plains were bowled over. Everyone looked up for the cloud or the rent in the heavens that would indicate that God had heard them.

So long as the fair seasons lasted there were few losses, aside from the tubas, clarinets, and pianos (which clattered and cracked, and had to be replaced almost daily by a ballet of helicopters). But during the harsh months — and it was a terrible winter — the hecatomb was massive. The oldest divas and baritones were the first to expire, with a final cooing. Rather than climb back down, the survivors, exalted by this commerce with the Invisible, clung to their peaks, braving the elements and the ice. The rock groups simply had themselves deposited on the loftiest tops and, with veins and noses chock-full of cocaine, they sank into the snow, howling blissfully. The few notes they played froze when emitted. Thus the great, white circus engulfed all the bands — pop, jazz, soul, reggae. The Rolling Stones, who had just reached the venerable age of seventy, completed their final world tour in wheelchairs on the peak of the Annapurna. They scarcely had time to strike the first chord of "Satisfaction" before they were overcome by the cold and turned into frosty statues. The classical music caste likewise perished, in perfect order and decorum. Refusing to don hats, gloves, or anoraks, all the stars of bel canto, keyboards, strings, and brass expired in tuxedos and bow ties. Certain performers froze to their instruments, falling with them to be skewered on needles of quartz or limestone amid a fracas of wood and brass. All these artists, congealed in iceberg perfection, with an arm or a leg sticking out from the glittering carapace of snow, looked like the jetsam of some ship

153

that was wrecked on the highest points of the earth. In the Alps as in the Andes, heaven had the last word; and it held its tongue. Mothers gaped in terror as their children, fresh out of the conservatory, took off, with a guitar or violin under their arms, to offer themselves in a bloodbath to the Great Indifferent One.

These ostentatious sacrifices ultimately disgusted God. He saw them as nothing but the pirouettes of a fickle people stricken with faith the way others are stricken with colic. God no longer believed in God: He would make a different world somewhere else, toss the dice once again. And He vanished into the cosmos. For their part, the pious and the devout, exhausted by a yearlong rumpus, threw in the towel. There was something vexing about God's disdain. The thesis that God was a snob spread abroad: "So we're not good enough for Him? Let Him stay put!" Meanwhile the allergy to noise increased. Nervous nellies strangled their neighbors for clattering a spoon, for coughing. Skillful businessmen, exploiting the troubles, vended slices of silence. Obligatory calm was decreed. Overnight the globe, which had been basking in a nonstop racket, regained its quietude. Who would now dare to try and trap God in a chord or a scale? People spoke sotto voce, birds held back their trills, flies barely dared to quiver. Wherever canned music was played, the volume was always low or the place sound-proofed. Nightclubs became as tranquil as churches. The Almighty had decamped; we would do without Him. Louis remained: that was the crux.

○   ○   ○

No sooner was Louis rid of the Supreme Being than our Delightful Fucker had to undergo a new ordeal: the presence of Lucia. It was not just the irruption of a lovely girl into a scholar's rigorist universe; it was the telescoping of two civilizations, almost two planets. This was what happened: Whenever the dancer came and twirled on Louis's palm, she coaxed and wheedled, captivating Him. He therefore asked her to appear every day. He nurtured great ambitions for her and planned to inform her at the proper moment. She showed no surprise, and her family encouraged her to develop this relationship. You don't turn down intimacy with a messiah. Who knows? He might help her out, get her a job. A kid of that caliber could pull all sorts of strings.

At first she was flattered by this attention from someone who was already rumored to be the replacement for God. She was not astonished that He was a baby. The Flabbergasting Minus was at the apogee of His renown — that sufficed. Everything was so new for her, so unwonted: the Kremer Castle (more closely guarded than a fortress), to which she took a taxi every afternoon; the lofty wrought iron bars flanked by sentinels in full-dress uniforms, their chests embroidered with the emblem of the Divine Child (an empty cradle); the lines of adoring fans (some had been camping there for months), to whom ushers distributed hot food and drinks; the crowd of babbling, gurgling domestics; the security men, wearing very tight suits and communicating on walkie-talkies; the majordomo, who, in a small electric car, picked her up at the gate and drove her up a long, plantain-lined garden path all the way to the Castle's perron; the gold and pomp of the entrance hall; the rooms she traversed, their walls covered with books up to the ceiling; the final library, a smaller one, its floor tiled with ancient leather volumes that they walked on barefoot; the two double doors opened by an electronic passkey; the long, narrow corridor that could be negotiated only in single file; and finally, behind a locked chamber, the Sacred Brownie's room, its shutters always closed, its windows thickly draped. She was always alone when she penetrated this room, at whose center a four-poster bed perched on a small platform surrounded by candlesticks and incense braziers. On that bed, drowning under curtains of gauze and muslin, sat the Mother, that mattress of fat, four years older than Lucia, mired in her pillows like a barge in mud, fanned by fly-whisking slaves with huge feathers churning up the almost unbreathable air. And, inside that female mastodon, enclosed like a kernel in pulp, lay the prodigy of prodigies, the pocket Einstein, the Holy Pineal Gland.

Lucia sat down in an easy chair, her image was videoed into Madeleine's womb, and Louis gazed at her. She didn't have to dance; all she had to do was sit opposite the enormous mammal (the slaves would slip away upon the girl's arrival) and converse with — or, more precisely, listen to — the child. Being watched without seeing made her feel queasy, and their first few meetings were torture for her. But she managed to pull herself together and soon deployed all her talents to appeal to the infant. By means of docility and coquetry, she eventually established a certain sway over him. She enjoyed certain privileges, earning her the enmity of the dignitaries of the Church: she could come and go as she pleased without being searched or questioned. In fact,

Madeleine, usually asleep, was the only person who showed her no hostility. The heavy, sweaty female seemed incapable of any sentiment whatsoever. Two armies could have torn each other to bits under her very nose and she wouldn't have batted an eyelash. And people could talk in front of her without apprehension: she neither heard nor listened.

It soon dawned on Lucia why the Philosophical Fly summoned her daily: He had taken it into His head to "fecundate her with His knowledge" — in other words, to dispense the Good Word to her. Toward what end? He couldn't tell her for now. Actually, Louis was planning to have her rule at His side in the womb, to enthrone her as the messiah's twin, His female double, a substitute for Céline. He therefore had to give her a crash course, apply the cramming method, of which He Himself was the finest practitioner. Too bad that in order to perform this task He had to put off the Moment of Revelation.

The girl didn't have a chance to accept or refuse. The bambino imposed His rule on her, and she complied without understanding, but reckoned on some future benefit. Every afternoon, from four to seven, the Supreme Schoolboy majestically assumed his pedagogical role. With his hands crossed behind his back, He opened the vast storehouses of His mind to Lucia, dictating dates, facts, and theorems in an abominably serious tone. Never for an instant did He doubt that she would be mesmerized by His magnetism, His aura. Supervising her on His monitor, He hauled her over the coals for the slightest inattention. She had to take high-speed notes in a big notebook and show equal interest in all subjects: particle physics, plate tectonics, the comparison of grammatical classes in the Semitic and Indo-European languages, the ethical stage in Kant and Kierkegaard. Louis, who did not respect the compartmentalization of knowledge (an infirmity reserved for mere mortals), lavished an all-around instruction on Lucia. She also had to recite the homework she completed the previous night after work. Every evening, before she left, He would greedily ask, "What would interest you for tomorrow, Mademoiselle: theology, linguistics, epistemology, genetics?" And the Super Show-off, caressing His cerebral peduncle the way one fingers a rabbit's foot, would pleasurably speechify in his anti-aircraft lair.

Lucia, steeped in respect and timidity, would obey. At eighteen, this girl, who had just managed to get her high school diploma by the skin of her teeth and was now taking dance lessons, found herself back in the classroom, treated like an infant by a sententious tot. Louis's voice had not changed — it hovered somewhere between a suckling's squeal and an oldster's quaver. He squawked more than articulated, and since His squawking was grave and unctuous, she had to choke back her laughter. Why did He force all this knowledge on her? What did it mean? After all, she hadn't asked Him for anything. She didn't understand one iota of what He taught her. His gibberish went in one ear and out the other. All His preaching sounded like reprimands, all his homilies like remonstrances. He kept iterating and reiterating, "Louis deserves Himself, Mademoiselle." She guffawed and dreamed of slapping him. Oh, how tiresome the Celestial Brat soon became! And, worse than tiresome, tedious. And, worse than tedious, as dull as dishwater. Oh, what a drag, what a sublime bore! Make Him keep quiet, for pity's sake, make Him shut His trap! He lectured her, hectored her, picked every last nit. And when He explained the differences between the Nestorian and the Monophysite heresies about the twofold or simple nature of Christ, she was overcome with an irresistible urge to take to her heels. Why should she care about an image quarrel in Constantinople, about the Reformation and the Counter-Reformation? And why shove foreignisms down her throat, why teach her *Weltanschauung* and *Zeitgeist*, since she didn't give a damn about having a view of the world or knowing the spirit of time? Oh, He was no fun at all, the little fogy. He was no champion of sweet talk and witticisms. Whenever she left His room, a throng of toadies and courtiers swarmed around her, eager to touch someone who had spoken with the Savior, who had been close to Him. She became a talisman in their eyes; they kissed her feet, ran their pudgy hands over her. Had they but known what she thought of that Divine Child of theirs!

She was soon fed up with His pedantry. She was not going to be pestered anymore by that grotesque Grand Panjandrum. And so she wore less and less to the work sessions, wrapping herself in bulky jackets or cardigans to avoid offending the faithful, but with very skimpy undies. And the Verbose Shaveling, caparisoned in His role of schoolmaster, was disconcerted — He had a hard time keeping His cool. He therefore turned over a new leaf. He washed before her arrival, and every morning He shampooed the thin bouquet of hair growing on the topmost protuberance of His skull; yet these precautionary measures were useless, since there was no possibility of her seeing Him. But above all, He no longer managed to achieve a meditative state, and He acted bristly toward His partisans. One thing and one thing only counted from now on: late afternoon between four and seven o'clock. The slightest tardiness on Lucia's part spelled torture for Him. By three P.M. He would already have ants in his pants. He squirmed and fidgeted, unable to read a line. The instant she walked in, the Little Runt began frantically jigging up and down. And when she left — "fled" would be the more precise word — He was incapable of buckling down again. He would review the session and reproach Himself for some blunder or other, all the while picturing Lùcia, her face at a slant, nibbling on her pen, fluttering her lashes, stifling a yawn, so far away in her nearness. He polished elegant phrases in His mind, pompous formulas that He was convinced would stun her. He prepared extremely intricate subjects to impress her with, looked forward to entertaining her the next time with the One and the Multiple in Parmenides — no, even more powerful, the Transcendence of the Ego: that was something she couldn't resist; she would stay on for at least an extra quarter hour, hanging on His every word.

But as Lucia sported progressively outrageous décolletés or a waist sheathed in a tight black dress that revealed long muscular legs, Louis found it more and more difficult to deliver His lessons. Where did she get that dizzying blouse, those flashy earrings? He was dumbstruck by the sight of His smart, chic, sexy pupil wiggling her hips, judiciously crossing and uncrossing her legs. What was this? He could barely speak: "My God, she's beautiful!" Then He pulled Himself together: " 'Euclid alone has looked on beauty bare.' There is beauty only in a concept; anything else is an illusion of the senses." He was at a loss — in the beginning, Lucia had looked so respectable, with her chignon and her dark suits. Why then was she wearing so much makeup now, with violet eyelids, glossy and aggressively red lips, bare shoulders, her hips in a miniskirt, or her legs in pantyhose so tight that it displayed every nook and cranny of her anatomy? Why those mischievous glances, those gestures of a smutty madonna? Louis, who believed Himself free of the senses, was desolate to realize how vulnerable He was to these worldly temptations.

And on the day, the disastrous day, that Lucia showed up in her simplest garb of all — a gaping T-shirt revealing two round globes with pointy tips and a bare navel, an admirable umbilicus at the center of her belly; and wide colonial shorts allowing glimpses of peekaboo black-lace panties — Louis discovered something intolerable for a pure mind of His ilk: the awakening of the lower parts. Yes, indeed: while He gaped His eyes out on Lucia's lures, something that had always been buried between His thighs surged uncontrollably. It was the most degrading phenomenon imaginable: five years of scholarship had failed to throttle His instincts! Now it was no use wearing silk loincloths that He changed daily; the cloth was bruised by the irruption of the bird perching on its branch. And the accursed animal left Him no peace.

What could He do to prevent it from soaring off? No doubt about it: the bird wanted to zoom toward Lucia, who, however, kept forgetting her lessons by the next day, stopped listening, and was a bad pupil. She would sulk through entire afternoons, lose herself in contemplating her nails, patiently buffing them into mini-mirrors that reflected the light. She answered in monosyllables, and when she was reprimanded by Louis, giggles came up from the bottom of her throat, galling the child like scratches on skin. Louis was flabbergasted: how could she not be interested in the problems of *Dasein* in Heidegger, in the faculty of judgment to legislate a priori in Kant, in the reasons for the waning of Buddhism in India after Emperor Aśoka? She pouted, squirmed in her chair, daydreamed, clock-watched. "My goodness — she's bored! No, impossible!" Once she even brought along a pretty snub-nosed girl of her own age, and the two of them kept guffawing and elbowing each other; but within an hour the friend, having dislocated her jaw, dozed off, and Louis asked her to clear out. He admonished Lucia, who shrugged. She expressed herself incorrectly, hated subordinate clauses, and juxtaposed disconnected sentences. She also had a knack for picking up street-smart words and ways — a hair-raising habit. Or else, to drive him up the wall, she would hyper-use predicate pronouns *ad absurdum*, repeating like a parrot "It is I, it is he, it is we, it is she!" One day she was guilty of a gross error in sequencing tenses, saying "If I was older." Louis exploded: she had no right to make such mistakes! How were they supposed to tackle the study of tropes, catachreses, antonomasias, and oxymorons if she could master neither syntax nor grammar?

o   o   o

Lucia failed to show up the next day and the day after, but never called. Louis went bananas. He rang her up. The girl's mother informed Him that she had gone off to rest after a sudden fatigue. She had left no message. Had she at least taken along *The Theory of Chaos* or *The Nicomachean Ethics*? Louis dispatched a few spies to monitor her home. He inundated her with telegrams in which objurgations vied with threats. He consoled Himself: she was nothing but a vamp, a louse smelling of musk and patchouli. Just who did she think she was, anyway? Did she realize Whom she was dealing with? But the louse irresistibly turned back into a goddess. Oh, what a living death, without Lucia! All the sagacity of the world could not replace the freedom of running after that palpitating creature. Damien and his wife, Ulrike, both of whom looked askance at the ballerina, begged Louis to give up His sophomoric behavior and devote Himself to His duty. He was so upset that he sent them away. When He could stand it no more, He penned a lengthy letter, revealing His goals to the young student. His intention was to share the Final Bedazzlement with her and to redeem humanity with her.

One week later, Lucia reappeared. The Ersatz Magpie's plans had left her cold. She found them somewhat jargony and muddled. The lectures resumed, but she dragged her feet. She felt terrorized by the Minuscule Torquemada. He now granted her a quarter hour of playtime per session. So the lessons, commencing with a highly erudite topic like the Invisible Hand since Leibniz, would end with a round of backgammon or Chinese checkers. One had to admit that the scoundrel was gifted, winning nearly every game; although He acquiesced very reluctantly to these trivialities. The ratio very quickly reversed, however: fifteen minutes of Spinoza was followed by an hour and a half of Scrabble or Trivial Pursuit. There was no way to get Lucia to study. She displayed a frivolity that bordered on indifference; she couldn't care less about the whys and wherefores. Louis was deeply distressed by her impulsiveness. However, His sorrows were only just beginning.

One day the beautiful bubblehead was up in arms. Louis had just explained — too rapidly, alas — the philosophy of Mani, the originator of Manichaeism, that dualist vision of the world subscribed to by the Paulicians of Armenia, the Bogomils of Bulgaria, and the Cathars of Occitania. Next, to divert her, He had asked her to comment on the Lutheran chorale in Johann Sebastian Bach's Cantata BMV 161: "Come, sweet hour of death; world, your pleasures are a burden, I hate your delights like poison, your joyous light betokens my doom." Lucia sat there all agape, shaking her head to and fro. She stammered in a blank voice, "Louis, You have no right to make me withdraw from the world; I haven't lived yet."

"My instruction is aimed only at sparing you the horror of life."

"Spare me? But living is a pleasure for me, not a curse."

"The pleasure of an ignoramus," the child yelled. "When you're as educated as Louis, these things you call 'pleasures' will seem like dodges to you."

"They may be dodges, but I look for them. Besides, they're all I know. And You're wearing me out with Your sermons."

"What! Louis shows you the way, and that tires you?"

"What good is all that knowledge? Does it make you any happier, any more cheerful?"

"Happy?" Louis was suffocating. "Why, Louis doesn't give a damn about being happy! Happiness is within any-one's reach, and Louis is promising you an uncommon destiny. A God, Lucia, has no right to share ordinary feelings. He seeks Truth and not the trivial little joys. That is why Louis is going to strip men of this existence, so that it stops burdening them."

"Just what are You talking about? You're depressing me with Your fancy blabber. I want to laugh, dance; and I'll have enough of an old age to think about the problems of Being and Truth."

"I thought I was clear. . . ." In his disarray, Louis had gone back to speaking in the first person. "Well, if you like, then we can certainly slow down the pace, and if you care to, we can dance between lessons. My little sister, Céline, taught me jive, rumba, and the rudiments of the mambo."

"Dance?" Lucia burst out laughing, and each guffaw sliced into the tot's brain like a shard of glass. "It takes two to tango, and You're just a baby, Louis. You only come up to my knees, and besides, we're separated by an invincible barrier."

"Science will reduce you to My size, and you can move in with Me. There's room enough for two. Once you try Mom's bedsprings — the softest seats in the world — then believe Me, you'll never feel like going anywhere else."

"I have no intention of locking myself up with You in a skin room. I left my mother ages ago, and I don't care to find a new one. And besides, it's all ridiculous. It would be best if I didn't come back."

"No, please stay, Lucia, I beg you. We'll talk, we'll talk about something else."

o   o   o

A person gets fed up with himself before getting fed up with others, and Louis realized that He could no longer stand Himself in the maternal cave. He had no idea how He could score points in the girl's eyes. For five years now, everyone had been worshiping Him, venerating Him, fearing Him, and those who had stood up against Him had paid dearly. But Louis had no sway over this girl. She was moved by neither His eloquence nor His fine speeches. In her presence, nothing was left of the Grand Pontiff baby. All at once He lost all desire to read. He no longer understood His earlier voracity, His former jubilation at aggrandizing Himself by appropriating the treasure of universal culture. He spent hours at his monitor, daydreaming and stargazing. How quickly the sandman showed up now, as soon as Louis began skimming a tome! To tell the truth, Louis was now bored by books — those wise places where wild or cruel actions are nicely stored on paper. Just why had He read so much, drudging like a convict?

It was as if a more complex datum were being introduced into His mind, modifying the overall enterprise at one fell swoop. Through that beautiful earthling, He could glimpse the arcana of a different, a richer life. Lucia radiated while He vegetated in His lair, suffering penance with His libraries and the whole cold storehouse of existence. An erudite and shivering canon, He felt like a pea trapped in its pod. The uterine Jerusalem was more desolate than an atoll in the middle of the Pacific. The Runty Robinson was bored. His courtiers no longer amused Him. He wished His mother would go outdoors, to a restaurant, so He could catch a bit of the world by gluing His eye to the peephole He had drilled in her navel. He pulled Himself together, exhorting Himself to buck up: "C'mon, the greatest men have had these moments of despair." He knew perfectly well what he had been doing here during the past five years — summoning all the cultures of the world to His private tribunal in order to dismiss them and terminate the aberration known as mankind. He would be the person about Whom it would be said, "He has read everything, even the books that have not yet been written." But He had so much left to discover; and when He saw the CD-ROM disks piling up at the foot of His computer, each one numbered for Him by his disciples and representing hundreds of thousands of pages, He was floored. And all this was nothing, compared with the stuff being published every single day in the world. He begged the hacks, the scribblers: "Stop writing! Get a hold of yourselves. Think about Me!" Bearing the weight of the world on His back was crushing Him: destruction is no less a restraint than construction.

The sequestered tot knew everything but had experienced nothing. If only He could sneak out incognito, leaving a stuffed cushion in His place, mix in with the squalor of human beings, their adulterated enchantments, and at the crack of dawn return to Mom's comfy nest! This would in no wise interfere with His resolution — quite the contrary. He felt such a powerful craving for the high seas! For lack of anything better, He papered the walls of His home with pictures of Lucia in a clockwise circle: Lucia sitting cross-legged, Lucia leaning forward, Lucia capping her pen, Lucia playful or angry, languorous or scowling. And instead of transmitting a page of the Talmud, the Koran, or the Gita, the multiple screens in His cockpit now showed the young dancer's pretty face. She replaced all the other landscapes, wiping out the false library and the thousands of immaterial books that had once decorated the uterine crypt. Lucia now constituted Louis's ground, skyline, and cosmos. However far He looked, He saw nothing but her. But with the endless Lucias whirling around Him in an infinite sarabande, He still lacked one: Lucia nude. And, to His great distress, once He imagined her stripped He felt His little reed poke its way upward, disarraying the neatly ironed folds of His loincloth. Believe it or not, Louis did not have one of those baby wands, arched like a sea horse and no longer than a faucet: His was a thick stick, a truly adult member the size of a forearm, its weight yanking Him forward.

Oh, the irruptions of His beast; oh, how it humiliated Him. On some days the barrier rose every half hour! The brainchild felt the little imperious alpenstock growing between His legs, drawing Him irresistibly toward the counterfeit Lucias like a finger obstinately pointing in one and the same direction. Louis asked His peepee, "What are you trying to tell me?" And its obstinacy kept Him from thinking. Once He even broke off reading Saint Thomas to plunge into one of those bawdy eighteenth-century romances that He so abhorred; and the risqué scenes, the ribald dialogue got Him so hot as to re-arouse His root, which turned a bright vermilion. But goodness knew that His desire, having never served a purpose, needed no spices and could be fed by the flimsiest pretext. He thought, for example, "Lucia should give Me her breast, pamper Me between her teats," and His burettes itched furiously, His flageolet pointed its scarlet nose. He reprimanded Himself: "A hero of the brain has no right to get a hard-on. Imagine!"

o   o   o

During this period He acquired a habit of which He felt ashamed: He relieved himself, looking at the reflections of Lucia. For this smutty business He employed a special custom-made glove with which He could touch and modify the images in relief, feeling heat and cold, smoothness and roughness. Thanks to this lubricious item, He could lift Lucia's skirt and thrust His finger into her undies. As His little serpent stretched and hissed, He took it in His other hand, stimulating it. Oh, my, oh, my, it had to come out, He couldn't stand it anymore. And when the carnal jewel arrived, it left all by itself, and He splattered the cockpit of His emotion while releasing the grunts and groans of an australopithecine. But then, furious about the fictive striptease, He ransacked the icons of the girl, tearing out her tongue, pulling out handfuls of her hair, poking out her eyes, perpetrating the same sacrilege on all the Lucias. This frenzy did not calm Him down: His brand-new lechery manufactured its own objects, and He saw the bodaciously busty beauties multiplying all around him, the thick-lipped, sweet-butted sluts inviting Him to lewdness. The apoplectic energumen drew His little pistol at the slightest mirage.

The knowledge that He would never have Lucia except in effigy drove Him insane. His view commanded imperious embraces and caresses. He had to have her right there, right away, and meanwhile He didn't give a damn about the "principle of all things" or "final causes." Alas, though twisting His problem every which way, He saw no way out. Even if He left His hiding place, He would come up against a further obstacle: size. In Mom, He could hold Lucia in the palm of His hand, but in real life Lucia could hold Him in her arms, because she was a good four feet taller and weighed three or four times as much as He did. It was no use recalling all the tales about the amorous exploits of gnomes and their aptitude for belly-lashings; He conjured up an awful marriage with Lucia, who would wheel Him about in a perambulator or carry Him on her back like a papoose. He would never grow any larger after these years of confinement.

Lucia jeered at His massacres, His torments. She had knocked the idol off its pedestal, and in less than six months at that! What a joy to have Him at her mercy, the tot Whom everyone regarded as a giant! A giant? A dirty-minded midget was more like it. For through Madeleine's belly, Lucia could feel a wave of libidinous appetite billowing toward her, which she found both amusing and repugnant. From now on she would see the homunculus under only one condition: that she would no longer have to endure His indoctrination. A single word about Kant, Max Weber, or astrophysics, and she would storm out, bag and baggage. And without further preamble, she began addressing Him by His first name — this fastidious baby, who had gone to seed all too quickly. He deserved no better.

Louis protested: "Oh, no, not that! I forbid you. You must show Me respect!"

She cut in: "Take it or leave it, Tom Thumb. Otherwise I'll leave!"

The Autocratic Brat didn't have to be warned twice. At the same time, he lost his capitals with her and his right to speak about himself in the third person. What misery, what a downfall! So this was where his unclean thoughts had brought him! Luckily their conversations took place behind closed doors. Were anyone to learn that he was nothing but a petulant piglet in his sty, and that a slut was totally dissing him, his mental prestige would suffer. If only she didn't let the cat out of the bag! What if he offered her money for her silence? But that would entice her to blackmail him — he would be precipitating a catastrophe by trying to avoid it. What a mess he'd put himself in!

Just as you tyrannize the people who attach themselves to you, so too do you attach yourself to whoever tyrannizes you. The more the stuck-up girl made him drool, the more subjugated the Skirt-Chaser felt. The messiah had been messed up by the Miss. She showed him neither esteem nor consideration. Nor did she respect Madeleine; indeed, she pinched her chubby cheeks, exclaiming, "So, butterball's still snoozing?" She whistled when the sleeper snored; she sneered in disgust, wandered around the room as if she were at home, bitching about the furniture, the decoration, the painting. She just loved blowing hot and cold with Louis. Alternately calm and disdainful, she tied him to a torture stake and did a scalping-dance around him. She deliberately chose the most futile topics of conversations, applying her makeup while listening to inept music on the radio, trying several different shades of lipstick, talking only about herself, noisily chewing bubble gum and popping enormous bubbles. She poured out her grammatical mistakes, making idiotic statements and provoking him constantly. She always dressed like a well-brought-up girl, but under the starchy young lady there appeared a different Lucia, who sported garters, a G-string, and a jaunty bustier that puffed up her breasts like an obus. She would then wallow in the debauchery of dirty quips, off-color allusions, and sleazy jokes. As soon as she had set the child on fire, she would leave, heading to a restaurant or nightclub with some boy her own age, "tall, handsome, well built, my kinda guy." And with a sweet smile she would blurt out before closing the door, "So long, fly turd."

At the peak of his excitement and suspicion, Louis would stay awake all night, agitating his tool and grumbling unseemly things. The next day he would dun Lucia with questions, trying to find out everything about the previous evening. The moment she sensed that his goose was cooked, that he was ablaze with desire and jealousy, she would apply the consummate act of understatement, hinting at elaborate dalliances, indecent cavalcades after the ingestion of some aphrodisiac. She had a knack for running her tongue over her lips, making her nostrils quiver, which drove the Little

Lecher wild. Then she finished him off with a few extra tidbits, which utterly floored and shattered him.

Oh, what fun she had with that chatterbox! She never tired of tormenting him; she would cut a few capers, and her whorishly saccharine charms would ravage the baby. She would say to him in languorous inflections, "You'd like to give me a l'il ol' kiss now, wouldn't you? Jump on me and plow me good and proper, huh?"

The child replied: "Yes, yes."

And she: "Aren't you ashamed, you foreskin seed, you canary prick — you know I'm not for you. I'm old enough to be your mommy, and you're old enough to be my grandpa. You're so clumsy, so awkward!" Mortified, Louis tried to at least learn how to blow bubbles with gum (he ordered some specially) and whistle through his fingers. He also wore a fluorescent collar and small twinkling insignia fastened to his loincloth. And he envisaged ordering several pairs of blue jeans from a tailor. It was time for him to dress, to become fashion-conscious. He resentfully recalled the time when Lucia had jokingly asked Madeleine to pay her for her baby-sitting. But no matter what she did, and above all when she mistreated him, his weenie itched and wriggled like mad. . . .

Until the day the lovely princess pushed things a lot further. She asked the hobgoblin for a bust photo — no more, no less. No one actually knew what the child looked like: in his portraits he was always concealed by a shadow. Like God, he wanted to remain faceless. He promptly realized what was behind Lucia's request, and so he turned it down. It was too risky. The girl deployed all her charm to convince him. First she swore she would resume taking lessons from him. Since Louis wouldn't give in, she promised to display herself naked in front of him. The offer was ineffectual. So she switched from seduction to threats. She harassed him, insulted him, and, at her wit's end, resorted to the most shameless ultimatum: either he agreed or she would never come back. And she would tell everyone that she addressed him by his first name like the filthy little shitter that he was. She stayed away for a whole week, until Louis buckled, exhausted with grief and anguish.

The photos were snapped by the ballerina's friend, a dandy with overlong hair, and had to be taken in secret to avoid waking Madeleine or alerting the security service. But the rules of the Castle had slackened; the dandy, who managed to get a dozen shots of the Astral Dwarf, both full-face and profile, assured him that no one but the three of them would ever see the pictures. One afternoon, when Lucia made a special visit, she opened an envelope that a messenger — with the complicity of the entrance guard — had left in Madeleine's room. Upon checking the first few prints, Lucia shrieked. She certainly had not expected an angel, but she had hoped for at least a roguish face. Instead she saw a wrinkled freak, a baby Methuselah with a prematurely aged mask. His cracked skin shone and a gray, puddinglike mass emerged from his head, dripping down his cheeks like whiskers. Louis looked like a hybrid of octopus and gargoyle, a sketch for some shape that never quite crystallized.

She wasn't just scared at the sight of him, she was sick to

her stomach. Dropping the photos, which scattered across the floor, she took flight. Louis yelled his lungs out:

"Come back, Luthia, maybe I'm not very handthome, but I'm tho thmart, tho thmart, tho thmart. . . ."

Louis was so terrified that he didn't realize he was lisping, and he banged so hard on the walls of his jail that he woke up Madeleine.

Eight

∽

THE BARBARIC PARADISE

Louis had unwittingly star-
tled his mother out of a delicious dream. In her dream
Madeleine was experiencing the idyll of two young
people — their meeting in a discothèque, their feverish conversations, their first kiss on the dance floor, their embrace at
dawn on a deserted beach — when, forcibly awoken, she
found herself brutally back in her usual state of prostration.
Once again she saw her torso in rack and ruin, her body
overflowing like a river in spate, the loosening fabric of her
skin. Madeleine would never be anything but a sack of
tough meat, a uterine bag. She was perpetually indisposed
by the effluvia of sweat and urine rising from her belly. For
five years now she had felt heavy, full of water, barely able to
move her legs, and she was so stout that she couldn't even
see her feet. Who had reduced her to this heap of blobby
flesh? A creep named Louis.

It was an atrocious moment when it dawned on her that
she had been led up the garden path and was losing her best

years. If this went on her hymen would grow back, transmogrifying her into a grotesque pregnant virgin. And that little swine was trying to lose his innocence with a stuck-up slut! It couldn't go on! She was overwhelmed by a desire to punish, as powerful as her earlier need to indulge. Louis turned her stomach, got her back up, gave her gooseflesh: he was a clump of thorns ripping her from the inside. If only she could dismiss him like a lackey! Or, even better, vomit him, excrete him! This time she would not make the same mistakes as long ago — she would act in darkness, silence. And with the help of a Castle guard who was completely devoted to her, she began by sending a long secret letter to Martha, Dr. Fontane's sister.

o   o   o

Lucia never came back. Even if she had wanted to return, Louis's disciples would have prevented her. Damien, dear Damien, so precious a resource in periods of tension, handled things smoothly. He sent the girl's family a nice, tidy sum with the stipulation that she never darken the Kremer door again. As for the shutterbug, he disappeared mysteriously, along with his shots and negatives. Lucia now despised Louis and was sorry she could no longer harass him; she refused to forgive him for his deformity and weakness, much less for those long weeks of compulsory schooling. A couple of banknotes would not reimburse her for the pain she had suffered. The mere idea that a filthy brat had bossed her around like a schoolmaster infuriated her, in retrospect. A creep that ugly was more than a lapse in taste, more than a moral error. Not only did she intend to discredit him with libel and slander, she also wanted to track him down in his very lair and make him cough up some money. Waffling between the fear of flouting Damien's ukase and a craving for revenge, she hit on a stratagem and took the risk of sending the baby a miniaturized videocassette.

A messenger delivered it to Madeleine, who promptly swallowed it, though ungraciously (she was fed up with being a mailbox), and Louis acknowledged receipt in her stomach. The child, eager to see the tape on his VCR, was frightened by the very first image. The dancer had swept up her hair on top of her head, gold hoops were flashing on her ears, and she was smiling enigmatically. She paused a bit before speaking.

"Hi, Louis, do you recognize me? We haven't chatted for a long time. You must be wondering what I'm up to. Watch and you'll understand. I always keep my promises. Have fun, kid. Enjoy my gift."

She was trying to sound playful and ever so slightly condescending; but her voice hesitated. This lack of self-confidence did not augur well. Some muted jazz started up with a nonchalant tempo — a duet for piano and tuba. The camera drew back to show Lucia dancing, barely moving, in a huge room furnished solely with a bed and chair. She strutted bare-legged, her feet in sharp, aggressive high heels; she was wearing an undone silk blouse and an overly short, black leather miniskirt with a belt of the same color. Still remorseful about his recent aberrations, Louis viewed the film uneasily; having vowed to throttle his impulses, he was terrified at the thought of even the slightest deviation from his oath. And somehow he was all the more upset because this amateur flick, blurry, off-center, and poorly edited, was disturbingly clumsy.

Peering nonstop into the lens, with a peevish pout that threw her fleshy lips into relief, Lucia, still moving, began by unbuckling her belt, which dropped to the floor. This simple gesture touched Louis more deeply than he expected. She crossed her arms on her chest, producing a dizzying gully between the two globes of her bosom, while the tapering fingers of her long hands denuded her shoulders. She then curtsied reverentially; by the time she straightened up she had, like a magician, partly opened her blouse to liberate one breast — a magnificent fledgling still warm from the nest. Louis switched it off with his remote. He would not tolerate such exhibitions. He was going to wrap the video up and send it back: "Dear Lucia, you've delivered this to the wrong address. Keep your contortions for the degenerates who surround you. You are not going to be my moral blemish." Ah, the gorgeous slut: what further scenario had she devised to drive him bananas? But he would have it out with her later; right now he wanted to know how far that perverse tramp's imagination would go. He could still return the cassette afterwards. He reinserted it.

Her blouse was wide open and halfway down her arms. Her two round breasts, quivering with a life of their own, seemed to beckon to the hands to knead them. Lucia caressed them like two kittens, squeezing them affectionately, pinching the nipples. Next, sliding her palms all the way along her hips, she undid the zipper of her skirt, which she drew down, unhurriedly, exposing large areas of her belly.

179

When a small, dark line appeared under her navel, a slender, grassy streamlet announcing a soft hillock, Louis felt the crimson rising to his cheeks. He yelled. As if she had heard him, the girl covered her bust with her hands, pursing her lips in embarrassment. At that very same instant the skirt reached her feet, and gracefully bending her leg, she dispatched the garment far away. Louis was atrociously aroused. All his fine resolutions vanished with that skirt. Now, everything happened very fast.

Underneath, Lucia was wearing black scalloped panties that narrowed into a thin band — almost a string — in her crotch. Gloriously licentious, with her heels clicking on the floor as if punctuating her gait with whiplashes, she strutted over to the chair and squatted on it with her back to the camera. She peeled off her blouse, leaned over the back of the chair, and unfurling the immense shaft of her spine, she curved her back and stuck out her posterior. The camera orbited complacently around this star, shooting every portion, down to the grain of her skin. Under the pressure of her glutes, the panties seemed ready to burst, to explode like an overripe pomegranate. She flaunted an exceptional physique, a firm, toned musculature, and two dimples dipped into the bottom of her hips. Louis thought he would faint at the sight of these splendors. He wasn't shocked — no, he was paralyzed, and he was forced to admit that this blindingly white, naked flesh was terribly desirable. He couldn't breathe. He ripped off his loincloth, and his corncob, which he had thought forever dormant, surged up, scarlet from its jangled nerves. No, not that, not again. Oh, the horrible display! She truly would shrink from no indecency.

The music stopped. The ceremony stretched on in an even more ominous silence. Lucia, as if it were the most natural thing in the world, lowered her panties down to the folds in her thighs, unveiling her entire posterior; she grazed the middle furrow, and for a moment Louis imagined that a black, lidless eye had just winked there. Before he could react, Lucia covered her buttocks again, got to her feet, and sauntered around the room — a superb, restless filly, strutting and flopping about with a disdainful expression. She came up to the camera, her thick lips outlining a kiss, and with a lewdness that sent Louis reeling, she whispered:

"Little king of scribbling, you've just admired my strongbox, my two eiderdowns of love, my two chubby Edam cheeses. But just wait, you little rascal, be patient. Open up them peepers — you ain't seen nothin' yet."

The baby had, alas, fully understood. His enormous penis, a monstrous turgescence, almost violet with congestion, unfurled even more, knocking everything out of its path. It had grown since its last erection, and Louis insulted it, reprimanded it, banged on it with a ruler. "Sit, you ugly good-for-nothing, sit!" He was going to yank it out like a weed. But try to reason with so capricious a beast!

Lucia returned to the chair, sitting down with her face toward the camera, her widespread legs resting jauntily on the top bars of the chair. The lens zoomed in on the black undies, which formed a blotch on the lower abdomen. Short, dense hair frolicked about the channel, and through the fabric one could make out a kind of muslin, a black, fragrant savanna. But the little cloistered prince was only at the starting gate of his martyrdom. Stripping wasn't enough for

181

Lucia. With one finger she drew up her panties like a theater curtain to reveal the barbarously luxuriant wound, the furry flower bed under which the umbrella shell of flesh, splitting down the middle, stretched out languorously. A bead of water moistened this landscape. Louis shouted, "No, no, you mustn't!" By way of a response, two other fingers — godsends — smoothed the vegetation in their turn and divided the sides of the umbrella shell, giving birth to a mute countryside that unfurled like foldouts between the pages of a book. Heavy blood-gorged tapestries spurted out, dropping in lazy pleats while a small, hooded, vermilion muzzle poked forth. New decors, opening upon other, more and more fabulous scenes, loomed behind the first ones. Louis barely had time to register them before the ebony blindfold of the panties removed those mysteries from his view.

Now the camera offered a close-up of Lucia's face, her eyes shining with lust.

"Little fly, if you could sniff my burning bush and sip me at my source, you would be drunk on the headiest perfumes in existence. If only you would roll about on my drenched petals, gently push your way through my gaping gate! Come, baby, lose yourself in me. What are you waiting for? Make me climb the walls!"

The cruel, the divine slut! Lucia's fingers writhed to and fro under the panties like snakes, giving themselves over to some outrage that horrified Louis. At times their disorderly motion lifted a corner of the veil, offering a glimpse of a forefinger bluntly rubbing those sumptuous tatters, with a sound like lapping water. Disarrayed by this aggression, the lovely black fleece resembled a clump of roses flattened by a storm. "Why is she tormenting herself like that?" Louis thought. "She's making mincemeat of herself." He gaped, cursing the fabric that hid too many things, catching only bits and pieces. His huge totem stretched toward the screen, eager to replace the fingers, to cross the soaked fortresses. As the scene grew increasingly precise, it became obvious that Lucia was immersed in herself, reducing Louis to the role of witness. The sublime creature had no need of others — she could love herself. This got the little outlaw all the more excited.

The girl murmured with great difficulty, "Louis, the golden age is in my pleasure and not in the weighty volumes in your library. . . ."

Her singsong was surprisingly ingenuous, with a touch of postdelinquent innocence.

"Paradise is the very thing that consumes a woman during the ecstasy of loving; the fire that burns her is perpetually reborn from its ashes, so that extinguishing it means rekindling it. . . ."

Finally, in a barely audible voice, she whispered, "From that summit from which she faints, the woman hears a secret that no one can listen to without dying, without dying — no, not even you."

Lucia was now on all fours on the bed, her head slantwise on the sheet, her rear perched high, as majestic as a throne. Her panties, yawning over her privates, simultaneously offered Louis the Sun and the Moon. Her ass was a blinding lens. He wondered, "Who's so intimate with her that he can film her?" and he was submerged in a billow of bile. All her jewels were there, spread out, with their own geography and facets. Oh, this delectable torture, those gluttonous gaps: remove these delights from my view, please, or I won't be responsible for anything. With the fingers of only one hand, the girl occupied every venue, demanding the same suppleness, the same docility from each one. There was violence in those breaches, a wild haste forcing its passage. The results must have been succulent, for a ravishing contraction petrified her face. She roared, sighed, panted; her eyes, half-shut, turned inward, toward a place that no one and nothing could reach. She was not just Eve the temptress, but a different kind of danger — female witchcraft with a terrible blend of total surrender and absolute distance. She was worse than shameful: she was untouchable. By inviting Louis into her private realm, she was informing him of his banishment. Although lascivious and akimbo, she still belonged to no one but herself. Her self-worship in that huge, empty room bordered on scandal. Her heavy breasts, her exuberant curves, her long thighs with their moist trails made up an unbearable tableau: it was a fusion of gold and honey. She trembled, tetanized, with a bit of saliva drooling from the corner of her lips. Her face, thunderstruck, was the image of all the sensual delights that Louis had rejected. He felt hopeless — his testicles rushed him forward, his legs buckled, and suddenly his two hands grabbed his hard thing and he started yelling:

"I WANT TO DESCEND, LET ME DESCEND, I WANT OUT! . . . "

For the first time in his brief existence, Louis burst into tears. Like the baby he was. While weeping, he vigorously shook his staff of life, which was emitting thicker drops, watering his cabin like a jet. He shivered, dog-tired, sated with pseudodebauchery. In the midst of sobbing he kept spitting at the screen, shouting, "I hate you, I hate you, I hate you all, you've abandoned me," and his tears doubled.

o   o   o

Louis could not leave. His disciples would never forgive him for such an abjuration — they might even try to assassinate him. Above all, he would never adjust to outside life. He was a cellar rat who could see in the night of the womb, but would be blinded by light. And besides, the world was more hostile today than five years ago: it was too late to descend into that brutal century the way a toreador swaggers into the arena, too late to romp about, go on a spree, rub shoulders with all sorts of people, be the darling of the ladies, a little wretch with a mop of tousled hair who is reprimanded and who makes them laugh. When the sun touched him it would reduce him to dust. He had remained in the waiting room of life, down in Mom's hold, like a valise that's been checked — and now the baggage room is closed. One can't be born old. And the little fetal mummy was wilting, smelling fusty and moldy. He had wanted to crash the party, gain centuries over his contemporaries. He had thought he could slip in between instants of time as between drops of water: but they had touched him more harshly than anything else, hurling him into very premature senility. Lucia had merely accelerated his decay, toppling him with a flick of her finger.

Even more serious, Louis was losing his mental abilities.

His prodigious memory, his peerless intelligence were mis-firing, verging on bankruptcy. Everything about him was precocious, including his senility. Even though he had been able to reel off, say, the names of every player of every soccer team in every country on the four continents, down to the third division, he now sometimes caught himself cudgeling his mind for the name of a goalie or a center-forward. His brain, that Babel continent with miles and miles of furrows in its windings, had been diminishing for some time now. The soufflé had been collapsing, the lofty minaret shrinking ever since he had grown a further horn, between his legs. At each erection, from now on, he felt his cerebral hemispheres retracting, and he was afraid of squandering his gray matter. It also seemed to him that the books were moving and chattering in him like a raucous aviary, and that the least intractable of them were dropping from the shelves, com-mitting suicide, as it were. He had read them in order to neutralize them — he wanted them to be embalmed like corpses in their coffins and not boisterous like children dur-ing recess.

As it happened there were just too many books, and Louis realized how much he hated them. The truth was that there were so many books that one human life would not suffice to merely read all the titles. He was worn out by their multitude, their vacuity, and the way they kept beating dead horses. He was tired of the same old stories, same old ideas, same old plots that kept returning from hundreds of years ago in barely different garb. If only every library could burn up, like the one in Alexandria. If only they had strangled Gutenberg in his cradle, thereby holding up the invention of printing for a couple of centuries — what a gain of time! Now whenever Louis began reading a text he was eager to finish it, skipping passages, whole chapters, galloping toward the conclusion.

Occasionally he felt a vague remorse. What if some essential element had escaped him in his wild scramble to cover everything? What if he had omitted the scholium of a Church Father, the obscure aphorism of a Tibetan monk, the marginal note of a Greek archimandrite who would have provided the response that Louis was so deeply hoping for? Had a moment's inattentiveness cost him eternity? Could he have stopped at the external meaning of words, forgetting their symbolic sense? Had he perhaps neglected a term or a letter that contained the truth about everything, the way a cell potentially contains the chain of all living things? And what if he had misread? What if reading always implies rereading? And what if — a dreadful prospect — he had to read every last copy of every last book, and in every language to boot? He just couldn't! His brain would explode like an overstuffed paunch. He had not drained universal culture — no, he had merely scratched the surface.

During the past five years he had plowed through nearly eight million tomes with a hygienic rage, but he had not written a single line except for some unimportant letters. In principle, after his registering the final word of the final opus, the radiant formula allowing him to grasp the totality would spurt forth spontaneously from under his fingers to be inscribed on his monitor. But when he sounded his mind, no click occurred. It was really no use racking his brain, he had nothing to say. Those millennia of wisdom and reflections that were supposed to settle in him like dew on a flower had left nary a trace. And now the Mole Baby was mixing everything up, unable to put his knowledge in order, rambling into a labyrinth in which Plotinus was confused with the Tao Te Ching, the Upanishads with Verlaine's poetry, and Denys the Areopagite with the Three Stooges. The full brunt of the corpses resting in the folds of his mind weighed down on him, upsetting his judgment. The devourer of pages had wanted to erect a basilica devoted to ink and paper in his head; now he was drifting without a compass, from century to century, like a skiff abandoned on the waves.

For a long time he had been only a presumption of a human being; now he had become a cul-de-sac in life. He had been neglecting himself ever since the little slut planted fire in his belly by telling him that he was a castaway from happiness. Gone was the quasimilitary regularity of his existence and the monastic austerity of his cell. This cell was nothing but a donnybrook: the apparatuses were kaput, the CDs were scattered about, some of them streaked and cracked, the fax and part of the telephone switchboard were broken down. Louis didn't give a hoot. He could no longer stand wallowing in the maternal backwater like a spoon stiffening in a cold sauce; he wanted to escape, and now he spent most of his time glued to the TV. Who said he would never watch a Western, a football game, a good whodunnit? He therefore demanded that a satellite dish be installed on Madeleine's bed (she refused to have it placed on her head), and his followers reluctantly complied. Instead of reading Confucius, Montaigne, or Byron, Louis now relished series, sitcoms, and game shows. Soap operas, flimsy melodramas filled him with guilt-ridden joy. He developed an insatiable appetite for that prattle, for plots as silly as their dénouements. He needed a little dumbness in a chemically pure state. He was delighted by the most inept trash; he gorged himself on the industrial stupidities produced in hundreds of thousands of copies throughout the world. The conquistador of libraries had become a shock zapper, a zombie of the audiovisual. During this period he at least forgot that his dreadful lair was so narrow, that the skin on his arms and belly was covered with thousands of minuscule letters — as if his epidermis were restoring the texts he had read, as if he were becoming a live palimpsest, a literary substance. Every evening he would go and wash off those ink shingles in a basin, but by morning another dense and incoherent tissue of characters had appeared. And whenever he switched off the TV, he could hear the volumes plunging into empty space from the top floors of his cerebrum, their pages flapping like wind-whipped sails.

Night was lurking at the bottom of his brain, but he experienced a fine remission. Terrified by his slovenliness, his disciples begged him to stand his ground, to persevere. As they were not allowed to enter Madeleine's bedroom, they installed a thunderous sound system in front of its doors and under the windows to the garden, and the amplifiers yelled out words of support and comfort. Damien plied him, urged him, swamped him with appeals. He even managed to beleaguer Louis's TV screens, reaching him on all channels and ordering him not to give up the ship.

"Why bother?" Louis objected. "I'm too old now."

"You have no choice," Damien cut in. "You have to do or

die." And his imperious, metallic voice left an air of indefinable menace.

Lost, isolated, Louis went back to his planning, resigning himself to the old challenges. His adulators persuaded him to undergo some minor surgery, and so by means of hooks they implanted a whole crown of silicon chips in his head, each chip containing several million superconductive filaments. There were teensy banderillas providing virtually a forest of antennas on his temples. And thus equipped, he plunged the neurons of young monkeys into the marsh-mallowy softness of his brain. His followers, via Madeleine, inundated him with fruit juices, amino acids, vitamins, anabolism boosters, brain stimulants. Above all, Damien made him promise no more filth, no more smut. Having stopped playing with his bat and balls, Louis gave him his word. He also attached a tiny bell on his rod, and it jingled at the slightest tumescence. Upon feeling himself harden, he would instantly cry, "Help, help, I've got it!" and with a long, sharp needle they promptly injected some bromide into the corpus delicti.

Louis also benefited from a transfusion of new blood from infants. This was a hasty, but effective, patch-up job. And though shrunken, shriveled, and sore, Louis experienced a brief renascence because of these prosthetics, a final burst of splendor. He shone magnificently and almost managed to wipe out his obsessive memory of Lucia. He was overcome once again with his biblio-folly: he exhausted the whole of medieval scholasticism, the entire cabalistic corpus, all of Japanese literature, as well as the bulk of research on the chemistry of metals. His adepts, anxious to quell any slanderous rumors (people were murmuring that the young-old monarch was gaga and babbling), begged him to deliver his statement. It was now or never. Cheered up by his recent mental feats, Louis complied, rediscovering capital letters and speaking in the royal "we." His Lilliputian Highness officially announced that It had attained the periplus of the Mind in fast motion and that It was going to clearly articulate that which the previous centuries had mumbled. The tiny atom of fissionable matter, buried in its silo of mucosa, was planning to pulverize the globe. All men and women were to prepare themselves for the Regeneration!

Nine

~

A RETIRING FETUS

As of the date of the known Apocalypse, the Phenomenal Joker enjoyed a resurgence of celebrity. Millions of leaflets dumped by airplane over the major metropoles trumpeted the event: in three weeks, Nirvana! The defeat of the old world was slated for the fifteenth of August, the exact date on which Louis, five years earlier, had refused to be born, to lend himself to the human comedy. A shudder went round the world: What if the Super-Microbe were telling the truth? What if everything were to be resorbed through the magic of a vocable? It was enough to shake even the biggest skeptics.

The house and property of the Speculative Knickknack were isolated from the rest of the country. Lookouts and crack shots on the roofs, as well as squads of guards, maintained a foolproof barrier around the child and his mother. Assassination threats forced Damien to resort to draconian security measures. Louis's self-mongering had exasperated the messianic hope. The Castle had become a powder keg, the target of all unbalanced minds.

192

The authorities, who had gladly cooperated with Madeleine ever since Louis sobered up, took the announcement of the Final Upheaval very seriously. That was why the wild beast refused to leave its cage: He was preparing paradise on earth for us. Cabinet ministers and responsible people bowed to a superior power, the power of thought: this peewee might be holding the reins of the universal fate in his hands. This time, gentlemen, no blunders! Eager to avoid repeating Pontius Pilate's mistake with Jesus, they gave instructions that the mother should immediately be granted the things she demanded. She asked for only one thing: the release of Dr. Fontane, who was then set free, after three years of incarceration. The unhappy gynecologist hurried to thank Madeleine; he brought along his red-eyed sister, Martha, who, her cheeks gullied with vales left by lifelong torrents of tears, stammered incoherent prayers of gratitude. The physician had aged, his myopia had worsened, and his prematurely white hair provided him with a grandiose and majestic mane. From her bed of misfortune Madeleine eloquently pleaded his cause to Damien and the principal elders of the Church. She reminded them of his past services, his judicious decisions during the first few weeks — thanks to which Louis had become the Highbrow Egghead that He now was. Her discourse and the doctor's ingratiating manners swayed even the most deeply rooted distrust. Madeleine supplied the coup de grâce by reconciling Louis and Fontane during a memorable public session. The doctor knelt down, and with an overwhelming humility he begged for forgiveness, which the Pitter-Patterer granted him on the spot: bygones were by-gone, and rancor was *déplacé* now that

193

the Total Renewal was only a few weeks off. And with a gesture of clemency that astounded the gathering, Louis made the gynecologist His personal physician.

Having thus concluded the peace and healed all wounds, Madeleine could lock herself in with Fontane in all quietude — and for hours on end, since his new promotion entitled him to such long tête-à-têtes. She communicated with him through brief notes written in a very simple code: each letter signified its immediate successor in the alphabet. *A* meant *B, B* meant *C,* and so forth until *Z*, which meant *A*. Fontane, while participating aloud in an innocuous dialogue, replied with similar notes, each interlocutor then destroying the other's messages. They had to forearm themselves against any discovery by the disciples, and especially Louis, who could spy on them through His multiple screens. Contrary to the Peewee Patriarch, who absolved people with might and main, Fontane had forgotton and forgiven nothing. Three years of prison had exacerbated his aversion: come what may, he had to eliminate the monster that he had helped create. He was flabbergasted to find Madeleine equally resolute. Her about-face was totally unexpected. Even Martha, between sobs, was siding with them. Louis had drawn a formidable hostility against His person!

But everything remained contingent on the success or failure of the fifteenth of August. It was too late to try anything before that date. The slightest misstep would arouse suspicion, dooming them to the most dire punishment. If Louis's prediction came true, they would be swept away with the others and awaken in a world where the words "reprisal" and "retribution" would be meaningless. On the other hand, if Louis's prediction misfired (and Fontane prayed that it would, since he preferred his vengeance over universal salvation), they would have to strike at the Saintly Suckling instantly, taking advantage of His confusion and the probable disaffection of His followers. Thus they had to stake everything on a fiasco.

Fontane, who examined Louis daily, was able to give Madeleine a bit of excellent news: the little Braggart was shrinking by roughly one millimeter per day. His fingers were contracting, becoming buds again, His nails were dropping off, tearing like paper, His limbs were atrophying, His teeth were loosening, His skeleton was reappearing in a filigree. And His skin was as black as if He had tumbled into a bucket of ink. He was fossilizing, returning to his embryonic state. It smacked of the miraculous: destiny was on their side; nature was punishing the Brat that had dared to defy it. A further stroke of luck: the cenobite's lair was a shambles — the eyeglasses that enabled Him to see inside His mother as if in broad daylight were shattered, and the numerous keys to Madeleine's inmost quarters were broken. Nevertheless, Fontane recommended circumspection and deference: Louis had to believe that they were indefectibly faithful to His cause. And, to set an example, the doctor pulled out all the stops, devoting himself incessantly to the well-being of the Perfect Braggart, thereby compelling Madeleine to outdo herself with caresses and cajolery for her son. She also terminated her activity as a professional sleeper: there was no time to doze; she wanted to experience the final days of creation with open eyes.

During the weeks preceding the Event, all sorts of

rumors were making the rounds. According to some, enormous, breast-shaped icebergs had broken away from the polar banks and drifted all the way to the Norwegian fjords, discharging torrents of milk far into the hinterlands and spreading a heady odor of maternity. According to others, angels with female torsos and baby heads had appeared in the western provinces of Canada, sitting down at the tables of certain families and placing two fingers on their mouths as a signal for silence. Whole villages had held their tongues ever since. None of this hearsay was confirmed, but as the Great Evening drew closer, it was almost normal for minds to slough off a bit of their rigor the way a magnet goes haywire near a magnetic field. The human race was on vacation, so to speak: work schedules were lightened, major projects were put on hold, and no one risked even the slightest forecast. Louis's proclamation had left all and sundry feverish. Every day, thousands of letters and telegrams arrived for Him: "Deliver us from the grindstone of life; emancipate us from the affliction of drudgery." Members of sects mailed Him charms, talismans, esoteric formulas, assuring him of their redoubtable power. Charlatans tried to steal a march on Him and, settling on makeshift rostrums, grimaced as they muttered impenetrable locutions. Their scowls and leers fooled no one, and with the help of blackjacks and alpenstocks the Divine Child's security personnel quickly talked them into leaving. Nobody seemed to take the end of the world tragically: weren't we going to resuscitate in wisdom, detachment, and serenity?

Louis paid no heed to these ups and downs. He crammed relentlessly, granting Himself only one or two TV soap operas a day. Being in a great hurry ("pardon Me, the Last Judgment is slated for next week"), He read only index cards and brief digests. Thus he ordered abridgements of *War and Peace, The Three Musketeers, The Brothers Karamazov, Doctor Zhivago,* and *The Remembrance of Things Past.* Why hadn't He adopted this method from the very offset? It was so much faster! Now He tackled Robert Musil's famous novel, *The Man Without Qualities,* abbreviated to ten essential pages: plot outline, analysis of main characters, innovation the work provided in its time, and helpful quotes. Get to the nitty-gritty, don't bog down in details, read at Mach 1, Mach 2 — that was His ambition. Likewise, He had no time to approach the musical masterworks one by one. All he listened to now was mixings — Beethozart, TeleSchuBach-Mann, MonteValdi. A software error had caused Him to mistake Zola for Dickens. Who cares about trifles? Brass tacks, brass tacks!

o o o

At long last, the day of reckoning arrived. Starting at the crack of dawn, tens of thousands of men, women, and children gathered at the crossroads of the biggest cities in Europe, America, and Asia. Giant screens were set up on each street. Since it was summer in the Northern Hemisphere, many people had slept outdoors, and the arteries of the metropoles looked like vast nomad camps. In Paris, all traffic ground to a halt. Ambulances no longer troubled themselves about bringing patients to hospitals: why bother treating them if Annihilation was only hours away? Madeleine and her son were resting in an armored cage at the center of the Castle's immense reception hall. The area around the cage was strewn with roses, carnations, and white lilies as well as nails, glass shards, and anti-personnel mines. Batteries of mobile cameras relayed everything, via all the satellites of the globe and the telecommunications centers of the principal armies. Numerous rockets were ready for takeoff in order to transmit the ultimate message through the spheres.

Louis had demanded that the scenic effects be kept to a minimum. Brahms's *Requiem* would be played softly, and a discreet lighting against a dark background would convey a sense of imminent abolition. The Perspicacious Scoundrel had groomed His appearance for Doomsday: He had spent a long time combing His pompon (only a single hair, in fact, as stiff as an iron wire), washing His body and His face, waxing the final piece of gray matter emerging from his head (that vestige of His exuberant flowering now no bigger than a young goat's horn), and exchanging His loincloth for some flowery Bermudas. And now, cross-legged, he sat there waiting.

The factories, offices, and high schools closed, and the zoos, barracks, and hospitals opened. Why maintain a semblance of order if both workers and soldiers, criminals and lunatics would be redeemed by virtue of a phrase? Certain storekeepers, who'd gone raving mad, were giving away mink coats, precious jewels, and deluxe watches and were hurling rubies and diamonds right and left: no hand reached out to grab them. Mirthful bankers were distributing whole sacks of big bills and emptying their coffers to the utter indifference of the passersby. On the verge of the upheaval,

people had lost all taste for lucre: the rich opened their
lovely mansions to the poor, serving them on their gold and
silver plates; hookers offered themselves gratis, but nobody
was tempted by this display of flesh; and bosses agreed to
astronomical pay raises. A joyous confusion reigned in the
streets: sworn enemies and angry spouses begged each other
for forgiveness; imprisoned murderers hugged their jailers;
wolves and bears, leaving their open cages, fraternized with
toddlers, who clambered on their backs; mothers gave their
last-born to lions or panthers, who licked them affectionately. An outburst of love and tolerance arose from the community of the living. The disciples of the Divine Child,
singing, waving banners, and distributing armfuls of flowers,
urged everyone to turn their thoughts to Him. The world of
misery and iniquity was about to vanish, the way a candle
blows out.

With a dramatic roll of a drum, the Fetal Nugget popped
up on all the screens on Earth in the early afternoon. A single
shriek of fear and trembling resounded from north to south,
from east to west. Howling children dashed into their
mother's arms. People had already known from hearsay that
Our Savior was no Adonis; but since this was His first public
appearance, they hadn't realized that He was so aggressively
ghastly. Damien, shocked by the cast of His features, was
sorry he hadn't hooded the Divine Child, as some people
had suggested. Louis was so hideous that viewers feared
they might get contaminated and disfigured just by looking
at Him. He had grown even uglier since the time that Lucia
had seen Him in photos in the maternal bedroom. The ring
of microchips on His head formed a veritable crown of

thorns, pasted to the flesh by nail-size drops of dry blood. His fogy-baby face, scraggy and toothless, was a site of abundant precipitation: His eyes watered, His nose ran, His mouth drooled. His skull produced a grinding noise as if a clockworks were straining to get going again. Next to His little cerebral tumor, His brainpan, now as flat as a helicopter's landing pad, sported a police light that kept flashing red and blue. The Shriveled Squirt looked like a prehistoric creature decked out in some cheap modern finery — all in all, the most alarming mishmash imaginable.

Disgusted, the televiewers closed their eyes. They had to reopen them: like it or not, it was this ignoble mask that was about to emit the Truth. A few superstitious souls voluntarily saw Louis as having the repulsive virtues of the garlic cloves that drive away vampires. He had started concentrating. Drops of sweat were beading on His brow; but He was oozing rather than perspiring, and a sticky film like that of a batrachian was coating His skin. His police light was spinning faster and faster. It was two P.M., the heat was scorching, people were seeking shade. Even the inhabitants of the Bering Strait, even the Eskimos on their polar cap were hot: they identified with the Ignominious Larva. Everyone found it strange that these notions of cold and dog days, hunger and thirst, would soon be invalid. In the universe succeeding this one, the temperature would always be the same, poverty would no longer exist, restraint and satiety would reign. In casting off their mortal coils, human beings felt an increased affection for them; they enjoyed the illusions of the senses. The most emotional people wept as they hugged and said farewell.

Louis, after initially triggering repulsion, gradually evoked pity. All was forgiven; it was for our sake that the Tot had become so ugly — He bore the stigmata of our aberrations on His countenance. His lips parted, He let out a soft cry, His face had a momentary spasm, He sneezed a few times. To make matters worse, He had a cold! The poor thing! Every mom spontaneously pulled out a handkerchief for Him. In the East, night had already fallen, while in the West, dawn was barely peeping. But for Louis's compatriots, twilight was gathering: it was becoming obvious that the Truth would be enunciated in the cool of the declining day. Now words of comfort were aimed at the Tortured Brat. His name was being shouted, people were calling upon Him for help. They wanted to be done with it, and all private anxieties were snuffed out in this collective suspense. There was something grandiose in the way this shriveled monster was stretching toward the Absolute. Doubt was no longer permitted: they were going to swing into a different time.

Finally, while polishing His encephalic candle as if to stimulate the synapses, the Sleazy Brat emitted a grumble. The televiewers shivered; they held their breath. His jaws clucked, His lips swelled, and a furry tongue slipped out. His eyes, glaring vacantly, exhaled a dark burst, and the little spike on His head, crimson from all the rubbing, stood erect like a firebrand. He was enveloped in a kind of phosphorescence, a radiant aura. He kept sputtering and drooling; if only He could wipe His mouth, it wouldn't hold up the arrival of the millennium! A tic warped His face, twisting it entirely to the left. He appeared to be soliloquizing quietly as if a superior force had taken possession of His buccal cavity and were dictating His incomprehensible parlance. The sweat gushed out of Him, and the heat liquefied even the specks of blood coagulated around His sagging crown of thorns. His nailless fingers, like a leper's stubs, hooked into one another as they reached toward His face. Further colly-wobbles emerged from His lips, a scraping discharge, and ears pricked up in vain to catch an articulate sound. A gaggle of hiccups came forth, a belch: Truth could not be far off; it was rising from His entrails, driving the air before it. Instead of shocking the listeners, this expulsion doubled the tension. Suddenly the tot's eyes evinced an intense distress. His pupils spun bizarrely; the whites showed. There it was — He knew! He was about to speak. Five billion individuals huddled together as if constituting a single person: within a second, they would be transfigured.

Louis had, indeed, achieved Illumination, that space beyond time where everything is to be wiped out. He nearly died. He embraced the entire panorama of the human adventure, distinctly perceived the Letters of the Burning Coal, the Ultimate Wisdom, the Alpha and Omega. This vision was unendurable. The shock triggered a short circuit in the depths of His brain, igniting a fire. For several minutes the televiewers, who had raised their heads, thought they saw something beyond the child's pupils, which opened like windows: whole shelves of books catching fire in a spontaneous combustion, thousands of pages and covers twisting and charring. It made for a beautiful blaze, a rutilant glow, and clouds of sparks. Next, a fine rain of ashes curtained the little fellow's eyes. Writhing as if racked by intolerable pain, he shouted in a cracking, wavering voice, "Help, help . . ."

Suddenly the TV screens went black. And all that could be heard was a tiny bell ringing, ringing with the regularity of a death knell.

o   o   o

Now came the moment when Madeleine and Fontane found themselves in a huge empty mansion, dunned by creditors and without a servant to help them. The ceremony marking the end of the world had turned into a riot: for an hour following Louis's fiasco, furious mobs had attacked public buildings. Their disappointment was overwhelming, and someone had to pay the piper. Any of the Divine Child's groupies who had not had time to slip out of their togas were lynched. The freely roaming beasts of prey, regaining their true nature, ripped open dozens of innocent throats. Everywhere scenes of pillage and destruction cast a gloom over that day. The Kremer house was assaulted by unleashed hordes, barely repulsed by the security men. One wing of the mansion burned to the ground, and Madeleine was terrified of being grilled alive. In half the countries around the world, a state of siege was declared for an entire week, and small gangs of agitators kept spreading lawlessness. Finally the anger subsided, and life went back to normal.

However, Louis's profanation was already spreading like an epidemic. He represented the inhuman to a repulsive degree — the summit of knowledge and erudition. Just as

He had been hated for His genius, He was now despised for His weakness. To shout "Help" at the threshold of the Golden Age — what a cop-out! The first thing he lost was his capital letters, like an angel whose wings are torn off. The ludicrous messiah appeared as what he was: a pretentious nonentity, a vile crook. The worst qualifiers were coupled with his name — that residue of a miscarriage, that toilet blob. People loathed him for having believed him, for having been duped by him. Many wanted him to stand trial. The Church — or at least its remaining battalions — tried to unite around the toppled god. With astonishing aplomb, Fontane seized control of the organization, mounted a top-level coup, and drove out Damien and the chief executives after dragging them before an internal tribunal, which blamed them for Louis's downfall. Next the doctor imposed such tough discipline, including spying and corporal punishment, as to disgust the final faithful. Seldom had there been a leader more intent on destroying his own troops, and Martha, no matter how hard she sobbed, was not the last to snitch and to strike blows. Finally, while pretending to justify the Divine Child, the physician kept making more and more finespun statements, which managed to exasperate public opinion even further against the little squirt.

This time they were fed up with his rubbish. Everyone trampled even more fiercely on the old hardworking tot, dumping truckloads of mud on his talent, his intelligence. Lucia attained a real success by telling a scandal sheet about her misadventures with the "Ignoble Virgin." She came up with a ferocious bon mot that was then heard around the world: "Louis Kremer? Nothing in his cranium, everything

in his crotch!" Donations dried up overnight. Ecstatic
widows, who would have squandered entire fortunes on the
Noisy Brat, turned their backs on him. At the Castle the few
remaining gardeners and stewards, still waiting for their pay,
disappeared with a portion of the furniture. And public
interest in the child declined. A few months after his TV
appearance, the media barely mentioned his name. His detractors tired of battering and vilifying him. He vanished
from the common memory amid general indifference. And
the blasé public went in quest of other stimuli for their
hunger for novelty.

The mother and the doctor had escaped by the skin of
their teeth! The little bugger had very nearly succeeded:
they had teetered on the edge of all-out chaos! In the thick
of night, Fontane, with help from his sister and a thug,
transported the enormous mother in a van to an extremely
isolated farmhouse they had rented. He intended to wipe
out their trail, escape possible prosecution, and, above all,
complete their work far from prying eyes. In this retreat the
doctor gathered a huge number of high-precision apparatuses, and as in the early days of her gestation, the still
semibedridden genetrix was stuck all over with cables and
loaded down with cameras scanning every square inch of her
belly. Microphones attached around her navel caught the
slightest puff coming from the brat. And even though Louis
hadn't breathed a word since the fifteenth of August, Fontane ordered Madeleine to drink from dawn to dusk, to drink
anything — champagne, vodka, brandy, wine — so long as it
kept the child in a daze. Anything that besotted and stupefied him was for the good. The doctor also injected a chemi-

cal cocktail of his own making into the mother's veins, a recipe aimed at dissolving the little parasite.

Groggy from the alcoholic vapors that he sniffed, still flabbergasted by what he had seen, Louis was falling to pieces. All he could remember was a flash of lightning that had destroyed him on the inside, an atrocious burning sensation at his temples that still persisted. His brain was breaking down, scattering into dust; all that now remained of the immense citadel that had once proudly towered above him were thin partitions filled with empty alveoli. The portion still alive, situated under the brain pan, endured the final, undulating flames, like the débâcle of a glacier, dragging along the rubble of an intense mental life. The tot was doubling back along the road of civilization, retreating from complexity to simplicity, from knowledge to ignorance, from the cortex to the rhinencephalon, losing his memories, his aptitudes, his reflexes. He could no longer articulate his native tongue, instead he stammered incoherent snatches of Arabic, Persian, German, Danish, Kirghiz. He had become the very babel and compendium he had wanted to transcend. He whimpered, passing from brief trances to low spirits, rearing himself up only to fall again. His head, still too heavy for the rest of his body, pulled him forward or backward depending on which way he was leaning. Incapable of getting up, he remained prone, crawling through the maternal vessel, creeping with the help of his worn arms and legs.

The pleasant pools where he had once splashed about were now brackish and slimy. The uterine sac was nothing but a miry slough; whenever he managed to hoist himself up onto an islet, obscene waves licked at him, and he barely eluded their suction. Everything was disquieting, terrifying; boiling geysers spurted from the ground, jets of acid leaped from the mucosa, pitting his skin, brambles ripped large slashes in him, and he bled black ink. He trembled and shuddered and felt constant thirst and hunger. Just a short while ago, Mom had been a palace of muffins and jams, a cavern of gingerbread. Almonds and pistachios, chocolate and marzipan had grown on the walls. All he had needed to do was reach out — the harvest had been rich and varied. But now, everything he broke off from the lining of the womb had a nauseating taste; he could munch nothing without throwing up. His moist hideout exuded the stench of abandoned markets, of decomposing matter.

And his prison had grown alarmingly; he measured the shrinking of his size by the changing scale of his lodging — he practically saw the landscape expanding in front of him. To think that his head had once touched the ceiling; by now it had receded several meters. A cathedral with terrifying vaults and dizzying walls was now towering around the tiny recluse. And about him he could dimly make out a terrifying moonscape bristling with sharp points and Cyclopean accumulations. He thought he heard footsteps in the darkness, furtive eddies; he spotted fierce eyes glaring at him. His computers, bogged down in the mire, were as huge as movie screens, the keys were paving stones and the telephones were tree trunks fallen across roads. The CDs stuck out of the mud like the gears of a broken machine, and one day the jagged edge of a disk sliced off one of his finger stubs. His visual acuity, weakened by the flash of revelation, had dulled. He guided himself by smell, by instinct. His incipient blindness made his surroundings appear even more menacing. Whirling clouds and blasting winds lashed him, knocked the breath out of him. If he shouted, his shouts died overhead, instantly absorbed by the immensity of the womb.

He was condemned to these lower depths, never reached by light. And the inside of his head was even darker than this murky basement; the gloom spread through him, merging into his very substance. Only a catapult could propel him far from this hole, eject him through his mother's mouth or nostrils. When he was down to the size of a mutilated tin soldier, he had just enough energy to pick up the receiver of his only working telephone — one last time, at the price of an outrageous suffering — and call his mother. Huddling there, trying to be heard, he yelled in an incoherent jargon. His mother's voice, clear and distinct, emerged from the receiver with the violence of a thunderbolt. She explained that she had grown and that he was still the same. She promised to send him new equipment adjusted for her new size. He mumbled a few raspy, disjointed syllables; she swore that he was her little genius, her phoenix. No sooner had she hung up than a dreadful racket exploded. Louis recognized classical music, but the volume was so high that the most melodious passages became razor blades cutting him up, slice by slice, flaying him alive. Above the chords, Madeleine said in an exquisite, urbane tone, "Listen to this Mozart sonata — you were crazy about it when you were little. And here's your favorite Schubert trio and your favorite Bach concerto." The child, killed by the very thing he loved, tried to flee, but his finger stubs were too teensy to cover his ears. He wanted to tell his mother, "Lower the volume, Mom, for God's sake, lower the volume," but the sentence died on his lips, the words amalgamated into a pasty magma. He was like a bug nailed down by a long needle, vainly agitating its tiny legs. This audio torture wore on for an eternity, without recess or respite. It was so agonizing that Louis wanted to end it all by throwing himself on the blade of one of the steel disks twinkling in the night. But not one of those friendly guillotines was closer than light-years away. So the exhausted homunculus dropped into the maternal marsh to keep from hearing.

It was too late. He had already thrust his head into the mud when all hell broke loose. A terrible deflagration shattered his eardrums and split his brain pan. The blast hurled him like a straw against the walls of his cave. A tornado churned up from the depth of his innards, devastating his body and demolishing his brain. And he sank into an interminable vortex.

o   o   o

Madeleine visibly deflated; she wept with joy upon losing her first twenty pounds. She evinced the same fanaticism in eliminating her fetus as she had shown in instructing it during her early months of pregnancy. An exemplary patient, she combined slavish obedience with a lugubrious rage that drove her to anticipate the doctor's orders. She kept endlessly exclaiming, "Purge me of that turd that's encysted in me!" The specific prepared by Fontane was a dwarfing molecule similar to the kind used for plants: strong doses would shrink any organism. The doctor had mixed in a poison that attacked the spinal cord, corroded the cerebral functions, and made the muscles friable. Madeleine had fits of cheerfulness upon receiving these drugs. She would burst into laughter, telling herself that she was reducing her son the way you reduce a beef stew. She began drinking every morning, anything — whiskey, cognac, beer, champagne — so long as every mouthful was a weapon aimed at the chancre rooted inside her. She never got drunk, for her rage kept intoxication at bay — indeed, a slight tipsiness reinforced her annoyance. With a well-nigh panicky impatience, she waited for the estocada. And when Fontane described how the insect was melting like a bar of soap eroded by water, she almost panted with pleasure.

One day, when the thing was not much more than a big wart, Fontane dealt the coup de grâce. Taking careful aim, he subjected it to the type of high-frequency ultrasound normally used to crumble gallstones and kidney stones. The mite exploded and dispersed in a thousand fragments. Fontane undertook the final verifications and unplugged the apparatuses. Madeleine was delivered.

EPILOGUE

On a July evening one year later, a young woman with radiant eyes was dining with a man on a restaurant terrace in a southern Italian city. She held hands with him, played with his fingers, laughed in fits and starts for no reason. She was well developed, with full lips and a bodacious bust. A long plait of hair, as shiny as a ray of black light, dropped down the middle of her back. She barely knew the man eating in front of her — she had met him on the train the previous day, and that was all she cared to know. Young and charming, he was the hero of the moment. He gave her longing looks, clowned around, and chided her if she failed to react when he addressed her by her first name. Saying her mind had wandered, she laughed all the harder and beamed mischievously.

Madeleine had changed her name to Laura, and she still kept forgetting it. To anyone who had seen her in her corpulent days, she was unrecognizable. She had changed from obese to bulky, and then to very svelte. A human being had resurfaced from the matron's envelope. The casing of fat melted to reveal a back, a belly, a bosom with a precise shape and contour. The two great trunks of flesh, which had not carried her in a long time, produced legs that were a bit stout, but not without grace. The puffy, porcine mug released a sweet face with big, curious eyes and the elusive bloom associated with youth. The metamorphosis was stunning. Madeleine's ordeal had made her almost beautiful, erasing the vacuousness that marred her adolescence. Gone were the angst, the existential terror that had rumpled her features. A different person — a foxy lady — was born, with just a touch of embonpoint and some adorably placed little wads. Her skin regained its elasticity, and all that testified to a jumbo past were some traces of weals on her breasts and thighs. She was as tall as before, but she would not have stood out among Northern Europeans or Americans. The sea lion, the couch potato had been transformed into a chic, attractive brunette.

And now something strange occurred: Fontane fell madly in love with this creature. She was his, this time, far more so than her son had ever been. Hadn't he resurrected her from the kingdom of impotence and immobility? Yes, he had brought her back to the world. And the little doctor, who had always thwarted the corruption of organisms, of blood and bowels, was convinced that he had won his finest victory over matter. Madeleine still had to be operated on by Fontane's friend, a surgeon, who would remove the microphones and apparatuses with which Louis had encumbered her belly — down to the tiniest screws, filaments, and circuits. Fontane also worked on detoxing her, gradually cutting down her doses of alcohol and giving her tranquilizers to help compensate. He then sent her to convalesce in the mountains and offered to marry her upon her return. Madeleine said she'd think it over. But the idea of getting entangled in new marriage bonds horrified her. She felt no gratitude toward the doctor: all he had done was repair his mistakes. And besides, he was too closely linked to the black years. His mere presence and the sighing phantom of Martha (Madeleine would gladly have twisted her like a winding sheet) would have revived the nightmare. So when the gynecologist and his sister came to drive her home from the mountains, Madeleine took advantage of a brief stop in a restaurant to rob them of a large sum of money; she gave them the slip and hopped the first train for Italy. Across the border she got hold of forged papers that identified her as a lab technician named Laura Wunderkind, a native of Colmar, Alsace. She knew enough about laboratories to get through any questioning.

At long last she was free, without ties or a past, restored to the community of her equals. Laughing at bygone terrors, she swore she would enjoy to excess the two passions that had been frustrated in her: love and travel. She walked the streets, proud of the looks darted at her: knowing she was attractive made up for centuries of forced ugliness. In every city, she gave herself to strangers, her appetite whetted tenfold by her memory of the days when she had gone to her conjugal duty as if to the slaughterhouse. Sensuality was the best revenge. She stopped in Florence, detoured through Venice, passed through Rome, and settled in a pensione in Naples. It was on the Rome-Naples train that she met the young Greek, with whom she communicated in broken English. That evening, after a light dinner in a trattoria, the young woman and her friend returned to their pensione, raring to make love. She undressed him feverishly, eager to be invaded, overwhelmed.

But inside her, a microscopic entity was lurking. This refugee from an old disaster was hidden under a blood clot the size of a ball bearing, and it was swimming toward her heart. And while Laura, athrob with pleasure, was murmuring tender obscenities to her lover, begging him to take her again and again, the scarlet pearl, navigating between purple and crimson, was racing toward its goal, guided by a single desire — to destroy — and by a single beacon: hate, hate, hate.